LOST
BETWEEN THE
STARS

LOST
BETWEEN THE
STARS

BOOK TWO OF THE
STAR STITCH CHRONICLES

Hazel Vale

HAZEL VALE BOOKS

First published by Hazel Vale Books

Ontario, CA

hazelvalebooks.com

Book cover design by moorbooksdesign.com

Inside formatting by Hazel Vale Books

Edited by Stephanie Hollingsworth - Lilac Editing Services

ISBN: 978-1-7780882-2-3 (paperback)
ISBN: 978-1-7780882-3-0 (ebook)

For Sers and Lavalle
Big shots who always stay busy, busy, busy.
And have the heart to keep us flying.

Prologue

The Obsidian 7828

Passengers jammed the hallways. Hurrying but having nowhere to go, they pressed into alcoves and stampeded toward the lower decks. Wynter Canmore nearly collided with a woman dressed in nightclothes. Clutching a purse to her chest, her terrified eyes darted around wildly as the man beside her demanded emergency gear from an equally terrified chef.

Wynter wished it were merely a prank, but those days were past.

The news had spiralled through the hex-system and beyond, rapidly gaining speed until it descended on the Obsidian.

The Monrovia—a rival ship—had exploded only two skips past the Polaris midway station.

Captain Ward should have been the one to inform his crew and passengers. He would have stayed calm and reassuring. Instead, a panic-stricken engineer had broadcasted it through all ten floors.

Wynter usually loved travelling between planets. Routines on the large luxury cargo ship were comfortable. The passengers paid little attention to her, and she understood the rules of decorum.

But this news of the Monrovia dispelled the notion of secure space travel. At that moment, Wynter wanted her feet planted firmly on solid ground.

Rushing through the halls, she knew what everyone must be thinking: if it could happen to the Monrovia, it could happen to the Obsidian.

The grand ship boasted ten floors of guild suites, cargo holds, extravagant passenger rooms, a pool deck, and every comfort possible. It suddenly felt small. The vastness of space between planets stretched wide in Wynter's mind.

On the bridge, she slid up beside Captain Ward. He didn't openly acknowledge her but shifted his weight, leaning toward her as he addressed the gathered crew, answering their rapid-fire questions.

"Yes, Rane has already agreed to run through a security drill. No, we don't have the same core. No, if it happened to our ship, it would be different. Yes, our lock system would work. No, we don't have details, but we'll know more soon," Captain Ward reassured.

He dispatched one group to check on the mid floor passengers and another to open the dining area, where they would post a list of casualties.

They left the bridge behind and reached an empty hall. Wynter swallowed a lump in her throat as her feet sank into the plush lavender carpet. She tucked her arm around Ward's, closing the distance between them. The soft lights dimmed, signalling the end of the ship's daytime routine.

"The captain of the Monrovia is a friend." Ward's voice shook and betrayed his own concern. The Monrovia was only one of the hundreds of cargo ships sailing through the hex-system, but they often crossed paths and shared docking orbits. "I talked to him last week."

The sweet smell of candied breads and cakes greeted them from the main dining area. They stood with the others as the lists came up on a large screen.

She noticed some of the tension leave Ward's shoulders. The Monrovia's captain topped the list of survivors.

Casualties flashed onto the screen. Only six dead.

A small number compared to the severity of the explosion. Still, too many.

Wynter read over the names and tightened her grip on Ward's arm.

Lady Cristelle, one of Valtine's most influential heiresses—who had recently travelled on the Obsidian—was dead.

The last time they'd seen Lady Cristelle, she had been horrible to both Wynter and Ward.

The surrounding crowd tightened in on them, their whispers filtering through the air unchecked.

"Lady Cristelle Inkton—isn't she your fiancée?" someone asked.

"I was never engaged to her," Ward said softly, a hint of regret in his voice.

Wynter took a step back, feeling a slight pull in her chest. In the month since Lady Cristelle had made an offer of marriage to Ward, the rumours of their engagement had been difficult to dispel, despite denials from both parties.

"What will this mean for the Idex summit?" another voice spoke up, causing another uneasy stir in the crowd.

The summit was still just a rumour, but Wynter knew it was only a matter of time. Poorly kept secrets regarding her unusual origins and the disappearance of a highly influential ambassador had caused a wave of disturbance throughout the planets. Voices that had been silent for a long time were now demanding to be heard. The explosion of a cargo ship and the death of someone as prestigious as Lady Cristelle would turn the hint of a summit into a reality.

The heaviness in her chest made breathing difficult. Was it guilt? Because Lady Cristelle would have been on the Obsidian if not for Wynter?

No, not guilt. That wasn't it. No one could have predicted the tragedy of the Monrovia. Wynter tried to sort out her feelings, but they were all twisted up into a deep sadness mixed with a sort of pity.

Wynter fixed her eyes on the names, longing for them to be different. It was a peculiar sensation to pity someone who was dead.

One

Lady Cristelle Inkton pressed her jewel-clad foot against the window. The glittering heel was, unfortunately, not large enough to block the floating severed hand.

She shifted her foot, but the fingers persisted in poking out from behind the tip of her slipper. The flickering red light cast the digits in an uncanny glow. Of all the wreckage scattered across the expanse, it was the only thing even remotely close to her, which was a terrible nuisance.

Parts of the Monrovia danced in front of her. It had been the largest cargo ship she had ever travelled on; now the sections and floors floated like tiny petals falling off a flower.

Cristelle spun the delicate vial that hung from her neck between her fingers. Pulling out the stopper, she dabbed the newly designed sky-lily scent on her wrists. A deep breath brought the light floral notes to her nose and provided momentary relief from the stale flux gases and storage blankets.

She adjusted the white throw over her skirts. It wasn't cold —not in the climate-controlled pod—but she was shivering, and the diamond necklace was like ice against her skin.

Lord Kent had suggested the diamonds were too ostentatious for a cargo ship. Bright red rubies weighed down her gown's fold-in pocket. She pulled them out and examined them. They were gaudier than the diamonds. The plan had been to parade them after the evening dinner, daring Lord Kent to comment again on her choice of jewels.

Lord Kent was the only other passenger with an Idex remotely close to her own, and he had spent most of the trip with her. He was stale and talked far too much about her younger sister, Lady Violet. It was terribly ungentlemanly the way he compared Cristelle's dark hair and complexion with her sister's lightness. He also liked to take jabs at how Cristelle spent her time. As heiress, Cristelle was an oddity, being so far away from home and accompanying her father's Inkton perfume cargo. Guild trade was barely acceptable for a lady with her level of Idex, even though it doubled her family's already vast income. But since her time on the Obsidian, she'd become less discreet about her interest in the company, even going so far as to look into the manufacturing.

Alongside the rubies, the hidden pocket held a cufflink she'd swiped from Lord Featherson and a hairpin from a forgettable lady. It was another low way for a lady to spend her time, but she enjoyed leaving the stolen items around the ship for others to find. The taking was the fun part. Now she was truly a thief, still having them in her possession. Her mother would banish her if she ever found out.

If only she could disapprove of the floating hand and make *it* go away.

She hoped it didn't belong to Lord Kent.

But no, it couldn't be. He had been on the other end of the ship, and she had been—where? She'd left the dining room to retrieve her rubies. Instead of rejoining the crowd, she'd descended to the lower decks to check on the perfume cargo. One of the vials she had stolen on Orion intrigued her, and she'd wanted to compare it to others. She thought she was alone when someone unceremoniously pushed her into the safety pod.

Cristelle hastily suppressed the memory. The ominous sound of the door locking, then the alarms sounding, and the terrible shaking—it was an ordeal not worth dwelling on.

Swivelling in her chair, she lifted the mounds of dress that the chair failed to contain. Layers billowed over the armrest and onto the floor. The dress was stunning, a cherry red gown with a shocking amount of fabric.

At dinner, the gown had made a statement. All eyes had been fixed on her.

And now here she was, drifting and rotating slightly apart from the wreckage, waiting for the rescue ships with only a severed hand to keep her company. It should only be a few days before she'd be back at the midway station. Thankfully, rescue ships were fast and designed for quick bursts in space.

Cristelle stood to explore her cramped surroundings. The compact safety pod was intended for unoccupied areas of the craft, and was a crude option for a distinguished passenger. Four chairs with safety harnesses sat under a low ceiling—low for her height at least. The silver panelling tickled the top of her dark curls as she stretched. Three doors lined the back: one led to a bathroom (of sorts), another functioned as a storage closet (although it was mostly empty), and the third was the hard exterior door she had entered through—or rather been pushed through.

Time crept as if the safety pod was languishing in a terrible dream. Eventually, hunger harassed her enough that she opened a ration pack. Whoever checked these lower safety pods hadn't replaced them in years. She wrinkled her nose and took a bite of the dried fruit bar, trying not to gag. After the failed attempt to eat a fruit bar, her heart sank, and her mood lowered.

Every six hours, the safety pod completed another slow rotation, bringing the arm and the wreckage back into view— the wreckage that was drifting further and further away.

The eerie silence stalked her for two more days. Cristelle nibbled halfheartedly on ration packs as she waited for the rescue ship's arrival.

As she completed yet another rotation, Cristelle's blood suddenly ignited. She could feel the pounding in her chest, the fiery anger. She stood, threw a horrid fruit bar onto the floor, balled her hands into tight fists and paced the very short length of the pod. The rescue ships had finally arrived. They cleared away larger sections of the Monrovia, and smaller rescue ships skipped across her view, picking up the cross section of floating pods.

Cristelle should have been the first one rescued. Her Idex, her vast wealth, and her land on Valtine demanded it. She would discover who had deemed cargo and other passengers more valuable than her and ensure they had cause to regret it. She sat. The chair bounced as she leaned forward to survey the control panel. Sophisticated programming meant it should have run without oversight, transmitting her status and location the moment she stepped into the pod.

One after the other, they collected the safety pods and parts and then disappeared.

Perhaps she was supposed to press an alert button, but it all looked foreign to her. The comm looked simple enough, but when she picked it up, it didn't have an automatic set of calls.

She hit the buttons, hysterically calling into it. It didn't even look like it was functioning. The comm hit the floor beside the fruit bar, and she kicked them both away. The pod didn't respond to her tantrum, but slowly floated around. She scrambled for something else to get their attention before the wreckage was out of her line of sight.

The lights inside her safety pod shifted again to morning, emitting a warm glow. Cristelle paced until her feet were sore, sleeping intermittently in the reclined chair and, for the next few days, did her utmost to rein in her anger, refusing to cry.

Too much time had passed. Even if everyone was already at the midway station, they would know she was missing.

The moment they realized she was gone, someone would come to find her.

By the fifth day, she discarded her dress, wearing only a white dressing gown. Undergarments were soaked in the silver sink, then hung over the chairs to dry. She could spot one of her shoes, but the other was hiding, playing games with her to pass the time. Her hair became an unmanageable braid. She left her diamond necklace on.

She spent all day waiting for the auto lights to turn from sunset into night, then back to morning again. Every time she woke, she calmed herself with the same information.

Spaceships spend months between planets, so a safety pod must sustain life for a similar length of time. There would be enough food for weeks—a month, if she was careful.

Those simple facts acted like an anchor as she held herself together. If she didn't, she wouldn't last a month. The walls were shrinking, already closing in. The ceiling felt lower, as if the surrounding void were compressing the ship.

Cristelle pulled at the tangled braid, focusing her fear into anger. She needed to be perfect and calm… and so help the ship that finally picked her up.

Two

Merrick Reid was careful to keep his tea away from the control panel. Steam rose and curled from the cup in vanishing wisps, the spiced scent lingering. A blur of shifting ink and flickering light danced across the narrow window as the Lark jumped past the stars.

He liked the design of the Lark. The dome-shaped room was simple. Twin pod chairs sat in front of the control panel on the lower floor. Smooth navy cushions displayed gold-capped buttons, and gold trim ran up and down the arms. The same navy and gold lined the columns that rose into arches and met in the centre. If not for the controls and the window, it could have been a comfortable living room. The upper deck held a series of closed panels and a row of chairs. His pilots, Sers and Lavalle, often resorted to using fold-down cots, despite having their own private rooms.

The trip to Orion had been a risk—and not without its losses—but it had been worth it, in more ways than one.

Merrick allowed himself to indulge in the brief flame of hope he had quieted long ago. They still had a lot of distance to cover and not a lot of time, but this wasn't a shot in the dark anymore. They finally had hope.

He took a slow sip, thankful for the rare moment to be on the bridge alone, knowing the soft ping of the alarms would bring the crew back. Even the unusual alert couldn't dampen his mood.

Jasper, his operations officer, was the first to reach the bridge. Dressed in all black, his midnight hair, dark features, and perpetually darker mood made his emotions difficult to gauge.

"Is there trouble?" Jasper asked as he leaned against the door frame. "I wasn't expecting any before reaching Tornillo."

Tornillo, a large space station between the hex-system and outer planets, would be their next stop. The massive floating city was weeks away, but they'd expected a quiet journey, other than scheduled salvage.

"What did you do?" Sers accused Jasper as he entered the bridge. The older man was wearing the same beige pants and black shirt that he always did. Only the top button was undone. His fashionable pepper-grey hair was styled to one side, unruly sideburns fluffed out in contrast. He grumbled something incoherent under his breath, then sent a polite nod, acknowledging Merrick. He took the left seat, folded his long legs under it, and spun toward the controls.

As expected, Lavalle arrived a moment after Sers, also wearing beige pants but with a red shirt he favoured. He was a little shorter than Sers and sported a ruffled moustache. Merrick didn't require uniforms of any kind, but Sers and Lavalle liked to distinguish themselves.

"Don't eat that," Lavalle said, handing a full plate of food to

Jasper's free hand and taking a biscuit with him to the controls.

Merrick raised a brow at the odd assortment of sweets, pickles, and rolled ham. Pickle juice slunk toward the fluffy cookies as Jasper put the plate down.

"What did Jasper do?" Lavalle asked, sitting down, his grin hidden under the powdered moustache. The gentle chime of the alarm stopped, and the tapping of buttons filled the void.

"I didn't *do* anything. I just arrived," Jasper ground out.

"You never know what's going on. Why are you on the bridge if you didn't do anything?"

Jasper turned to Merrick, who took another sip of tea, waiting for the last scan to come up.

"My scanner is picking up something a few hours out," Merrick said calmly.

Lavalle and Sers leaned forward. Lavalle's silver moustache twitched as he expanded two of the three-dimensional screens and overlaid them. Then a third.

"Only my scanner," Merrick added.

"Only your scanner—hmmm," Sers mumbled to himself.

Merrick had developed the recent enhancement to recognize ships with comparable cloaking technology. As far as they knew, though, no one else had it. Merrick had upgraded merely because he could, not because he thought they needed it.

"I'm not even sure there's anything there. Look. Regular scans show nothing. But overlay Merrick's—there—what is that?" Sers asked. The four men fell silent.

"Can we afford to stop?" Jasper asked. Time was on everyone's mind.

Sers leaned back in his chair and looked Jasper up and down

as if he was asking a stupid question instead of a completely relevant one. He handed him a datapad. There weren't many who would talk to Jasper the way Sers did. Jasper was officially on the Lark as the operations officer, but his natural talents leaned in a more lethal direction.

"It's in proximity to the Monrovia explosion," Sers added, ignoring the earlier question.

Merrick scratched at the stubble on his chin. Why would something on the Monrovia have cloaking tech? Or perhaps it was a problem with his newly invented scan. It wasn't as if he had tested it yet.

"It's too close to the Monrovia wreckage to be a coincidence," Lavalle said. "It's drifted some, but still within the blast horizon."

Jasper handed the datapad back to Lavalle and pulled a double blade from his hip sheath. He spun the black knife between his fingers, concern etched between his eyes.

Merrick weighed his options. It was along the salvage route, which required it to be cleared. If someone had his tech, whatever they were hiding was likely unsafe—but not knowing might prove an even bigger risk.

Lavalle and Sers were prepping navigation to make the detour but waited for his order.

"I want you to be prepared to dump the cargo if anything goes wrong," Merrick said decidedly. He finished his now lukewarm tea and turned to Jasper. "I'll let the rest of the crew know we have an unplanned retrieval."

Merrick quickly assessed the problem before him. This might be a useless endeavour if it turned out to be nothing. But if it was *something*, cloaked wreckage was unheard of and, therefore, dangerous.

Thankfully, the Lark could handle anything space threw at her.

Three

Merrick tucked his long knife into the side holster of his stone-grey overalls. After checking in with his crew, he jogged down to the loading dock.

Jasper was at the railing, gazing down at the double layered containment unit. The main airlock brought in scrap and space junk and was strong enough to withstand a minor explosion. Once sealed, the secondary chamber would open, allowing access to do a full check before exposing whatever they'd retrieved to the rest of the ship.

The Lark stopped above the object. Hull doors opened. The magnetic scoop grabbed the piece of wreckage and brought it in.

The first set of doors closed.

Merrick and Jasper stared for a moment, then Jasper reached for the control panel across from him, sounding a quick alarm throughout the ship.

"That is *not* wreckage," Jasper said.

They were used to picking up space trash or dislodged panels. Larger items were usually satellites that no one had bothered to take out of space. The junk was interesting only to Merrick, the scrap wasn't worth much. However, Valtine courts and guilds alike paid well to keep their flight paths clear. It was a job not many signed up for, and they were compensated accordingly.

They'd never picked up a safety pod before.

Pods weren't salvage classification.

"I don't like it. There's no way they would have just left this behind."

Merrick waited for the atmosphere to stabilize.

"We follow regular protocols. Until we know more…" Merrick stared at the pod. It looked dead. Backup beacons or a dozen other ways of being noticed were silent.

"Let's go see what we got!" Merrick said as the lights turned green, indicating that decontamination was complete.

Disconnecting the interior panels, Merrick turned the latch and hooked up his datapad to diagnose the issue.

"It appears that only the exterior systems malfunctioned. The interior atmosphere is intact. This is strange—pods don't use thrusters like this. They would have sent it far from the Monrovia wreckage." Merrick's voice trailed off as he inspected the ship for signs of cloaking technology that would have tricked regular scans. If it was anything comparable to his, the technology itself would be hard to detect.

The exterior lights weren't the only problem; the door was jammed. Like someone had completely rewired the entire thing. When he finally rigged the door to release, it hissed as stale air seeped out of the capsule.

Merrick was not easily surprised. His life on Koros and then sailing between the outer planets had taught him to be prepared for anything. Despite himself, Merrick jumped at what came next. Before the door had fully pulled back, he saw a hand with delicate fingers, then an arm, a shoulder, and finally the rest of a body squeeze out of the tight opening. A woman recoiled from the shuttle as if it were lined with thorns.

Jasper was quick, clearly not as shocked as Merrick, and caught her around the upper arm.

She was tall, wearing a thin white underdress and a grey blanket slung over one shoulder. Bright sparkling shoes covered with jewels dangled from her fingers; a balled up pile of red fabric bunched under her arm and trailed behind her. Her dark hair was a knotted mess on top of her head like tangled tree roots, and a diamond necklace hung sideways around her neck. She stomped on Jasper's boot with her bare foot, which would have done little to hurt him. Regardless, he released her, allowing her to flail herself in Merrick's direction.

Instead of fists, it was a lash of words as she stepped toward him.

"I want my dress washed and pressed. It's five layers of silks, Valtine silks. It must be done by hand. I want to speak with your captain immediately and lodge a complaint." Her voice shook as if she was struggling to control each word. The shoes slipped from her fingers and clattered to the floor. Barely looking at the two men, her eyes darted wildly, fingers clutching the gown she had demanded be washed.

Merrick wiped his dirt-covered hand on his coveralls and held it out to her. She looked at it, horrified. He let it fall back to his side.

"And I'm hungry. Please inform your chef that I'd like cortivals and wine brought to my rooms," she said. She looked close to collapsing. Merrick stepped forward to steady her, but she backed away from him.

"You heard her, Captain," Jasper said as he flicked the blade between his fingers, deftly letting it cross over every other knuckle. Jasper's demeanour surprised him. He should be, at the very least, concerned for the woman's well-being.

"I thought you didn't like calling me Captain," Merrick stated, trying to figure out what to do about the woman as well as Jasper's odd behaviour.

Jasper didn't like titles. Merrick wasn't too keen on them either, but it was hardly the time to point that out.

"Captain?" The woman pulled at the grey blanket that threatened to slide off her shoulder. Her eyes narrowed.

"Merrick," he stated carefully.

"I am Lady Cristelle," the woman said, as if it carried a great weight.

Which it did.

Lady Cristelle was dead. Merrick kept his face passive and glanced at Jasper. A flicker of something was quickly masked on his friend's face, something he wasn't going to share in the presence of this woman.

They had read the name a few days ago on the list of the dead from the Monrovia. She should have been listed as missing or lost. Not dead. She couldn't be Lady Cristelle.

Merrick expected Jasper to be more concerned. For more than one reason, they couldn't run an Idex scan on the ship to verify who she truly was. Their location would be picked up, and everyone on board would be flagged. A person's Idex was in their blood. Everyone was born with it, inherited from their mother in their own unique coding. It was trackable, traceable, updatable, irreversible, and never marked as dead without a body.

"I'm not sure what's going on, Stelle, but we'll get this sorted out," he said, trying to sound reassuring.

Her cheeks turned scarlet and puffed slightly, like she was building up a scream. She reached out her hand to slap him, but he stopped it midair. Shock registered across her face. This close, he could smell the stale perfume that clung to her. Her eyes looked hollow and haunted. Despite her shaking, she squared her shoulders and pressed herself closer.

"*Lady*. I am Lady Cristelle," she said. Merrick let go of her hand, aware he'd deposited a line of grease across her palm.

Four

Cristelle had thought the safety pod was failing, so when she finally saw the inside of a ship from her little window, panic flipped to relief, then anger.

When the door opened, there were no medical staff or stretchers waiting for her. Bright lights illuminated the immense hull. Cristelle stumbled forward, trying to regain control of her thoughts, fearing it was a dream and she was still stuck in the safety pod.

Two men stood in place of the grand welcome she deserved. The one claimed to be the captain and called her *Stelle*. Stelle. Never in her life had anyone addressed her without her title.

"I will not be treated like this!" Cristelle exclaimed, doing her best to keep her voice from shaking. Like a butterfly with one wing, the emotions fluttered and flapped wildly in her mind. Grabbing the one that was most familiar, she went with the clarity that anger brought her.

She tried to slap him, but he grabbed her hand. His reflexes were lightning fast, and his was the first touch from anyone in almost a week. He let her hand drop, and the cool air quickly replaced the momentary warmth. The red dress slipped from her tight grasp and puddled at her feet.

His forehead was knit with concern instead of interest or disdain. She scrunched her nose and made a show of inspecting him from head to toe.

He was not a captain. This had to be a dream. Dressed informally in grey coveralls, his hair was dark and shorter than what was fashionable. There wasn't a single wavy lock, unlike the current style most men favoured. The stubble on his chin gave him a rough look—not polished or acceptable for polite society.

The other man was older, although his age was hard to guess. His midnight-black hair was pulled back into a small knot, and he carefully inspected the pod she'd just escaped from.

Lifting the dress off the floor, the so-called captain straightened and, instead of trying to hand it back to her, he folded it over his arm.

"I want to be taken to my rooms. I need a shower and—and food." Her voice wavered. It was the second time she had asked for food. She wasn't even sure she could stomach cortivals, but anything would be better than the ration bars.

"We need to wait for the decontamination to finish. You can sit—"

"I don't want to sit." She stomped her foot, wincing as it made direct contact with the floor.

"If you'll excuse me, I need to talk to Jasper," he said, walking the short distance back to where the darker man examined her safety pod. She tucked the blanket tighter over her chest and looked around the large room. Row upon row of storage units lined the far wall outside the double dome system. A walkway with a railing ran the length of the room three floors up. If this was a cargo ship, it was a useless waste of space.

She swallowed, then banged on the door of the containment unit. Movement in her periphery caught her eye as a young woman appeared on the upper deck. She pranced down the thin silver stairs toward the enclosure. The woman, who couldn't have been over twenty, waved enthusiastically at Cristelle.

Cristelle pinched the inside of her arm, trying to wake herself up.

"Hold on Ava; it's not safe yet," Merrick said into a comm, coming up behind Cristelle. She could feel the nearness of him; this was not a dream. There was someone standing with her, reminding her she wasn't alone.

The secondary sweep finished and the containment panel opened, allowing the excited Ava to enter.

"I didn't know we were picking someone up! Why didn't you tell us? If I'd known, I'd have brushed my hair," Ava said. Dusty blond hair hung in limp strands around a pretty face. Large oval brown eyes and high cheekbones would have made her a beauty, even by Valtine standards. "Actually, you look like you need a brush more than I do. There isn't a room ready, but I'm sure we can—what's wrong, Jasper? Who is she?"

Jasper was shaking his head, trying to get Ava to stop talking.

"Ava … this is Stelle. We don't have a spot ready, but we'll get one cleaned up right away," Merrick said, his voice irritatingly calm.

"I think she needs a shower first. Were you in there?" Ava asked, pointing to the safety pod. "I'll show you the showers."

Cristelle was ready to properly introduce herself when Ava excitedly turned on her heels, expecting Cristelle to follow.

"Are there any other belongings we need to get from the pod?" Merrick asked when she didn't follow Ava to the showers.

Cristelle stared at him, rooted in place, unsure of what to do. A lady would never have accepted this kind of treatment. Tears pricked at the sides of her eyes.

When she didn't respond right away, he cleared his throat.

"Stelle?" he said again.

"Lady Cristelle!" she blurted, trying to regain her composure. "I will not allow you to address me so informally. My Idex goes back—"

"A lady?" Ava exclaimed, turning back to them, eyes wide. "On the Lark?"

"No one here's going to be calling her *Lady* anything," Jasper said, earning a glare from Merrick.

Merrick took a step towards Cristelle, and she backed up closer to Ava.

This was a joke, a terrible joke. She spied the gloves that were tucked under his arm and gaped at them. A captain didn't wear work gloves. She looked around the room again, taking in the size, the bins, the machine that was still connected to her pod.

"What kind of ship am I on?" Cristelle demanded, her hands knotted under the blanket.

"The Lark's a salvage ship." He sounded proud of it.

"No, no, no, no, no …" she cried in disbelief. She should be on a rescue ship with medical staff, a personal modiste with fresh gowns, someone to help her with her hair, and a chef—at the very least. This was a particle ship—a scrapper ship—and she was being treated as if she were space garbage.

The truth hit her, rocking her back on her heels. This retrieval had not been planned. No one had come for her. No one had missed her. They had all left her—rotating in that cramped pod—to die alone.

"I know this is a bit of a shock. We're a bit surprised ourselves. I'll show you to the showers, then introduce you to the rest of the crew." His words slammed against her fear and fury, and she spun out of control.

"Introduced to the crew?" Cristelle gasped. "Do you know who I am?" She might be stuck here for a few days, but to talk to the *crew*?

"I think you're lucky to be alive," Jasper shouted from behind the safety pod.

Five

Cristelle was led from the chrome and clear-domed area through a secure door and into the ship's living quarters. The wide hall with doors on either side was where the Lark stopped looking like a salvage ship. It could have been one of her country homes or a row house on Orion—or a mix of all the homes she'd ever lived in. Silver-and-gold papered walls faded into a panel of elaborate paintings with silver frames. Oddly-shaped coloured lights glowed white and blue, with every fourth casting a rosy hue. The floors were wooden planks with multicoloured runners.

At the end of the hall, stairs curved up in a spiral. Each step was a different floral pattern of cold black metal that reminded her that her feet were bare.

When they reached the top, Cristelle could see the closed doors lining both sides of the hallway. The soft scents of coffee and laundry mixed, reminding her how far she was from home.

She held her head high, noting all the doors and paths, which weren't many, and observed Merrick intently.

For a scrapper, he carried himself surprisingly well and there was a concerned look in his eye when he glanced at her. Ava talked nonstop, as if she'd known Cristelle her whole life, and Jasper followed behind, glaring sullenly at her.

Merrick opened a door, which led to yet another brightly lit room with blue and green-tiled walls.

There was a row of sinks. A row! Four sinks with large mirrors hanging above them. The same blue and green tile decorated the floor.

Cristelle shuddered at the inadequate aqua-blue bench. There were things about her non-rescue she'd have to accept, but there was no way she could use a community shower.

"I want to be shown to my rooms! I want my own shower!"

"Ava, why don't you see what you can find for a change of clothing?"

"I don't want clothing!" Cristelle yelled as Ava hurried away from them. Jasper followed, leaving her alone with Merrick.

Merrick opened a cupboard with a frosted glass door and handed her two stark white towels. They were fluffy and slightly warm.

"I should explain how this works," Merrick said, leaning past her toward the shower.

"I can figure it out on my own," Cristelle said as she brushed him off. She hated the way her voice came out sounding desperate. She wanted to be alone—needed to be alone—but worried that when he left, she'd finally wake up from this nightmare of a rescue only to find herself truly alone, still on the safety pod.

Merrick waited, as if he was going to say something else. Cristelle pressed her lips together and tried to slam the door.

It didn't slam but slowly decompressed before it finally closed. Frustration and fear mingled. If she was going to remain safe, she needed them to see she was in control; but even the doors were working against her.

Her blanket slid to the floor and she took off what was left of the only clothing she had. A deep breath filled her lungs as she stepped into the solid silver tube. It was tight. She could almost touch both ends at the same time with her arms stretched out. An elaborate display of silver dials winked at her, and she wished she had let Merrick explain. Backing herself up against the wall to avoid the spray, she pressed one dial and then another.

Nothing.

Cristelle stood staring at the panel as the minutes passed.

It couldn't be difficult. Trying again, she pressed another little round disk and a rush of water poured down on her. The tube was too small to escape, and the door wouldn't open. She tried another dial, but the stream forced out an icy blast.

There was a sound from outside the tube, and the water reduced to a drip. Cristelle shivered. The water had chilled her through, dispelling any notion that she was dreaming.

"There's a series of six dials. Pull the one on the far right first, then hit the second on from the left. It'll come out warm," Ava said from the other side of the door.

Cristelle followed the instructions, bracing herself for the onslaught of frigid water. The cold rush hit her, then dissipated as the warmth mixed in with it. She relaxed under the stream as Ava let out a wave of one-sided conversation.

"I brought you some clothing, but you are much taller than I am. And I think you must be wider. How wide are you?

Jasper said I shouldn't bother worrying too much and to just find something. When you're done, make sure you hit the far right button. It'll turn all the jets off. Once the water has drained, the door will open. Make sure you don't take too long. Merrick said to tell you to not take too long."

Then she was gone again.

Turning her face into the warm stream, she let it wash off the days in the safety pod.

Cristelle had no intention of listening to Merrick and would take as long as she wanted. A large ball of soap suds bubbled and slid off her fingers and swirled down the drain. She let the soap soak into her hair again and re-lathered her body for the third time.

The water turned chill, then stopped flowing completely.

She hadn't hit the button to make it stop.

The water shouldn't have turned off.

Her hair was sudsy, and little white bubbles clung to her shoulders and splattered down her side.

Cristelle stepped out of the tube, then back in, and tried to restart the shower. A splash of water hit the wall as she stomped her foot and yelled at the faucets that refused to obey her. She got out.

A warm towel soaked up the suds from her skin, but there was little she could do about her hair.

This was worse than dirty; she was soap scummy.

A pile of clothing littered the bench outside the shower. Cristelle held up a pair of light-blue pants and grimaced. Not only were they too short, there was no way she'd be able to fit her curvy hips into the narrow band. She set those aside and then almost cried in misery as she picked up the other ones and immediately tossed them. Hidden beneath the pants and loose tops were a few dresses: a pink day-dress with rows of fluff around the bottom, a worn sage-green evening gown, and a simple lavender gown with pearl trim around the scooped neckline. Cristelle donned the lavender, tucked her sudsy hair into a towel, and bit back a sob. She was cold and miserable and hungry.

Merrick was waiting outside in the hall. He was leaning up against the door as if it was a normal day.

"It stopped working," Cristelle said, keeping every strand of hair tucked up into the towel.

"It'll be hot again in an hour," he said and led her down the hallway toward the sleeping quarters.

The room was compact. There was a bed pressed against one wall and trunks were stacked along the back. There was little room for anything else. Cristelle recognized Jasper and Ava. The third man she hadn't met yet had cinnamon-brown, unruly hair. His smile was unnaturally wide. Holding up a red blanket, he shook it, then bent over and laid it on the bed beside a table with a plate full of food.

"This is Ruse. He's a mechanic," Merrick said. Her formal introduction to the salvage crew.

Ava waved again and held a small sweep, turning it off as it sucked up a bit of dust.

"Ruse, this is Stelle—"

Cristelle let out a growl of frustration. She wouldn't argue with a salvage captain. What did it matter if they called her Stelle? It didn't change who she was.

Ava and Ruse put the last few items down, making more room for Stelle to enter. She pushed past them and flopped down onto the nicely made bed.

She turned her face toward the wall, feeling the itch of drying soap and covering her head with her arms.

"Get out. I want everyone out of my room!"

They left, but the moment they were gone, she wanted to call them back. She didn't want to be alone. But aside from Ava's wide eyes and innocent smile, it was clear no one wanted her here, and no one cared who she was. Merrick had been polite, but reserved. Jasper looked dangerously irritated, and the newest crew member—Ruse—well, Cristelle knew a forced smile when she saw one.

She swallowed a lump as heated voices echoed in the hallway beyond her room.

Unable to decipher what they were saying, she counted to ten, waited for the yelling to stop, then sat up. They might not want her on the ship, but at least there was food.

A floral printed bowl held fresh grapes, cheeses, and an assortment of other treats. She ate everything.

Only a few days. She could answer to Stelle, talk to the crew, and survive. She wasn't alone, or dead, even if she was talking to scrappers. Only a few days, and this would all be over.

She curled up and closed her eyes and let sleep take her.

Six

The arguing began the moment the door closed. It was clear everyone had something to say, so Merrick moved the gathering to the bridge, where they could vent their fears without being overheard.

Sers and Lavalle didn't care what happened, as long as they were left alone to do their jobs. As far as they were concerned, a lady wouldn't be half as bad as Jasper.

Jasper confirmed her identity as Lady Cristelle, and his dark expression dared anyone to ask him how he knew. Ava wanted to know everything about her; Ruse didn't weigh in on the arguments but was eager for their next salvage, encouraging them to focus on the task in front of them. Jasper suggested they toss her out the airlock at their next stop, earning a moment of silence and contemplation as the crew considered the horror and convenience of such an idea.

Sers openly mocked Jasper's fears about having a lady aboard until Ava flicked his ear. Ruse crossed his arms over his chest and fixed his blue eyes on the screen that showed their next retrieval.

The Lark was not a welcoming place for a titled lady.

When the last of the murmurs died down, they all looked to Merrick.

"We need to press on," Merrick said. "We have a schedule to keep, and Ruse is right—we need to focus on doing our job. She's an unexpected guest, but the Lark is capable. For now, we stick to our side of the ship, and I want a watch on the bridge at all times. I don't care if she's a lady or a penniless servant. It's been seven days since the Monrovia explosion. She needs our help. Besides, she's supposed to be dead; no one is looking for her."

Silence followed him off the bridge.

Merrick made his way to his shop to think and come up with a plan that didn't put the Lark or his crew at risk. He took his seat at the workbench and dismantled the shower timing dial. He should have fixed it months ago, but no one ever complained about needing long showers. The coil was rethreaded and a fresh chip was put in.

The solution to one problem often came to mind while he was fixing another. Stelle was a problem, and the solution wasn't straightforward. Unfortunately, nothing came to mind while he worked.

"What do you really think?" Jasper asked, joining Merrick in his shop. Jasper picked up the red dress from the side bench and tossed it to Merrick.

The piles of red were soft under Merrick's rough hands. He ran his fingers over the clasps that held the back of the dress together. Small wheels clicked together, making a rose pattern. It was a clever use of the threaders. His understanding of fashion was lacking, but this was expensive.

"The clasps are a unique style."

"Not the dress."

Merrick tossed the dress beside a bundle of wires and focused on the timing mechanism in the small dial.

"I see you're finally fixing the shower," Jasper said dryly.

"Have you ever heard of someone being reported as dead without proof? It takes a full ten years of absence before they can mark Idex codes as inactive. Even then, without a body, they still aren't marked as dead," Merrick stated, not looking up from his work.

"No, and we shouldn't be the ones to bring her back to life." Jasper paced the shop, knocking little piles of clutter with his toes at every pass. "I came all the way out here to avoid people like her."

Merrick picked up the dress again and shook off the bits of wire. One of the rose clasps clattered to the floor. They couldn't change course, and bringing her all the way to Tornillo was a risk.

What he could do is fix the timing dial on the shower, and the lights on the lower deck that were stuck on a funny shade of green. He could reach Tornillo on time, then he could bring the Lark and Ava safely home.

"We're on a set course. Besides, how bad can one lady be?" Merrick asked, only a little afraid of the answer.

Seven

Stillness. The Lark felt eerily still, as if they weren't moving at all.

The climate control in her room was too warm, and she was stuck to her sheet. The dried suds in her hair fell like snow onto the quilted blanket. She shook her head, shedding more white flakes.

Stelle rubbed her eyes and took in her small surroundings as the tightness in her chest unwound. It was a curious little room. There were no lavish themes or decorations, only basic items. The bed was comfortable; and she noticed the small chair and desk tucked beside the stack of trunks and boxes.

It was smaller than anything Stelle had stayed in before. It was smaller than even her dressing rooms. Stelle thought of complaining and demanding a larger space, but she had a feeling it would do little good. And there was something about the room that amused her. It was the kind of room her mother or her sister Violet would have refused to step foot in. Well, they'd never spent a week alone in a pod. She doubted they'd have handled that as well as she had either.

Sweeping the quilt onto the floor, Stelle did her best to flatten the creases of the dress and made her way to the showers to fix her hair.

The door to the showers was open, and tools littered the floor. The soles of dark-grey shoes protruded from the doorway, and as Stelle got closer, she could see legs—one was bent in a funny direction—and a hand reaching across the floor toward a knee.

Skirting around the tools, she inched her way in until Merrick became fully visible. He was sprawled on the floor in front of a little panel outside the shower. He grabbed the pliers near his knee and twisted the two red wires together.

Stelle studied him for a moment and wondered what her friend Lucy would say about the ruggedly handsome captain fixing a shower. She missed Lucy. Everything about this would have been bearable with her there. Lucy would have perceived Stelle's undeniable attraction to Merrick. She couldn't imagine anyone not being attracted to him. And then Lucy would have probably staged some sort of event to get Stelle on the floor beside him. But Lucy wasn't there and Stelle had no inclination to act on her straying thoughts.

"Will this take much longer?" Stelle asked, hoping to startle Merrick. He finished with the wires, pushed them back into the space behind the panel, and half sat up, leaning on one elbow. Stelle did her best to not notice the way his shirt pulled over his well-muscled arms.

"It needs to be tested—did you want to do the honours?"

"I'll wait," Stelle said haughtily, folding her arms over her chest.

Merrick piled up his tools, then turned the shower on from

the remote outside of the tube before closing the control box.

"You can shower as long as you want now," he said with a gallant bow and then stepped past her. "I'll show you around the ship when you're ready."

Despite having unlimited shower time, once the flakes had transformed back into suds and sunk safely down the drain, she didn't want to stay in the shower. She was more herself—more relaxed—and had spent more than enough time alone.

There was a small basket on the sink ledge with *Stelle* scrawled on a piece of paper. It was only a few days, she reminded herself. She could be Stelle. Maybe it would be fun?

She had always wondered what it was like to live in such a simple way, and Lucy would not believe the adventure she was having.

Inside the basket was a brush, a large pair of red socks, and a few more dresses that looked closer to her size.

Stelle worked a long braid, curling it around the base of her neck. After admiring herself in the mirror, she opened the door to a waiting Merrick.

She was expecting to be shown to more galleys and comfortable alcoves and places she could sit—the usual boring ways to wait out her time. But he was showing her everything else.

Stelle was enchanted with the unique ship but hid her enjoyment with a serene smile. It was larger than she had first suspected. She noted the rooms Merrick was telling her about and all of the ones he walked past without mentioning.

There were three floors in all. The midlevel held the living quarters with the rooms and showers; it was closed off from both the cargo bay and the bridge.

They descended a set of stairs. Merrick went first and held her hand as she reached the last two steps. The lower level was open to the cargo bay at the back, and a large open workshop took up the back of the hull. Beyond that, Stelle assumed, were engines and storage.

Merrick's workshop was her favourite. Despite the rest of the ship being tidy, the workroom was filled with boxes and clutter. She had never given much thought to things lost in space. A long desk displayed broken lights, wires, and tiny parts. Stelle stepped over a few boxes and inspected the odd parts.

Her red dress lay abandoned, tossed over a chair, with wires draped over it. She reached out to pick it up but pulled her hand back. Thoughts of the Monrovia crept in, thoughts she had tried to keep away. The sirens, the sounds. Being pushed into the waiting pod.

She didn't like the feeling as it snaked up her spine and made it hard to breathe. She buried it inside, deep into her chest, and pasted that serene smile back on.

"They pay you to spend months between planets looking for junk?" Stelle asked, turning away from the work desk, ignoring the pounding in her chest.

"We have a contract for certain areas and known items to retrieve. But the radars locate other items, and depending on our route, we stop. We pick up all sorts of space junk." He winked at her.

Stelle stared at him, lips parted in shock. No man had ever dared to tease her. She failed to think of a clever retort before Merrick left the shop, suggesting they get something to eat.

The last stop on the tour was the third-floor galley. It was sizable, similar to an entertainment deck on a regular cargo ship. Thick carpets rested on dark wooden floors. Black tufted reading chairs gleamed with brass trim. The room functioned as an open kitchen, dining, and sitting room. A long table was bolted onto the floor; the solid wood top gleamed. An array of glittering lights dangled from a support beam that ran the length of the ceiling. It stretched from the kitchen area all the way down to the lounge.

Ava and Ruse were sitting across from each other at the table. Ava was startled and stood up when Stelle entered. Ruse was harder to read. His brow was drawn together, but he offered a forced smile.

"Would you like tea?" Ava asked. Stelle was going to say no, even though she wanted a cup, but Ava was already moving toward the counter. "It's probably not as fancy as what you're used to, but we do love our tea on the Lark, and I think you might like this blend."

Ava flicked a switch on the wall where a tall curved copper pot was attached. It hissed and steamed in seconds, and Ava pulled it back, then poured it, shifting her weight from one foot to the other.

Stelle waited, trying not to make eye contact with Ruse. He appeared friendly enough, nicer by far than Jasper. But she was unnerved by the way he watched her.

Once the tea was brewed, Ava pressed the pine-green pottery mug into Stelle's hands instead of setting it down for Stelle to pick up herself.

"Oh, I couldn't possibly," Stelle said out of habit, but Ava was already sitting back in her own seat.

The first sip was exquisite. Like honey and spice. Careful to not let her pleasure show, she scrunched her nose. Pulling out her own chair, she sat down and swept her knees under the table. Back straight, she wrapped her hands around the mug.

"Well, it's warm," Stelle said mildly. "When is lunch served?"

Ruse exchanged an uncertain look with Ava, who shifted uncomfortably.

"We're all on different schedules. You can get what you need when you need it, but I had Jasper make up some plates while we were taking a tour of the Lark," Merrick explained.

He placed a plate in front of her, then grabbed a second plate for himself. Steam rose from the pasta and buttered bread, and fresh apple slices fanned the side. Ava continued to drink her tea, not bothered that they were eating and she wasn't. Stelle picked up her fork, balanced it delicately in her hand, and took a bite.

Ruse pretended to not be looking at her, but Ava watched her closely.

"More tea, anyone?" Ava asked, breaking the awkward tension.

"I can get it," Merrick said. He stood and placed a hand on Ava's shoulder, and she smiled up at him.

It was such a familiar gesture. An uncomfortable knot tightened in Stelle's stomach as she watched him pour water into the kettle and set it to boil.

This was the oddest ship she'd ever been on. Everyone was at ease, but something else lingered in the air. When the tea finished brewing, Merrick refilled Ava's mug. Stelle almost interrupted the pour to remind him to serve her first, but the mouthful of bread stopped her.

"I like your necklace," Ava said into the void.

Stelle let her hand rest on it.

"She meant it as a compliment," Jasper said, entering the room. "I realize you're far from home, but around here we say thank you to compliments."

"Don't tease her," Ava said.

Stelle was certain Jasper wasn't teasing.

"Is it real? I've never seen stones this large before."

The clasp opened easily, and Stelle ran her fingers over the jewels as she took it off. It was a gift from when she'd turned sixteen. She had received emeralds first, as was tradition, but she'd wanted something bigger—something better—and had demanded diamonds. No one had even questioned her. It felt like a lifetime ago.

She felt as though Jasper knew the story by the way he was looking at her. Jasper held himself with a little too much decorum, Stelle noted. It was something years of education would produce and time could never fully erase.

Wordlessly passing the necklace to Ava, she smirked at them both.

"Are you truly a lady from Valtine?" Ava asked, slightly in awe. She held the jewels up, letting the light hit them. "I've never met one before."

"Never?" Stelle asked. She almost added that she'd never talked with menial crew members before either.

Ava handed the jewels back. They looked huge in her frail white hand.

"You were on the Monrovia? That must have been scary. I've never heard of anything like that happening before. Do you travel often on those ships?"

"I wanted to follow the cargo. My family owns a

perfumery," Stelle said, making it sound perfectly normal. She waited for the usual comments about her involvement in guild trade.

"I didn't think ladies worked," Ruse said, his eyes deliberately focused on the tabletop.

"I don't work. It's a hobby." The lie rolled off her tongue with ease. It was work, and the polite society of Valtine didn't like it. She knew no one could force her to give up her passion for the perfumery, but they'd tried. Her own father had tried to bridge the gap by having her offer for Captain Ward of the Obsidian. Like her, his Idex was flawless, even if he was a captain.

Her time on the Obsidian hadn't produced an acceptable husband, but it had been fruitful in other ways. She'd helped her friend, Lady Daye, which was worth any cost to her own happiness. And she'd joined with Lucy to bring Captain Ward and the seamstress Wynter together.

"You're on the wrong ship to insult people who work," Jasper said.

Stelle was ready to argue that she hadn't insulted anyone when the soft ping sounded throughout the Lark. Merrick, Jasper, and Ruse all left quickly.

"I wonder what we're picking up," Ava mused, dropping the dishes into the sink. She rushed to clean up the mess and then grabbed Stelle's hand. "Whatever it is, I doubt it'll be as exciting as you."

Eight

For the next three days, Ava was her constant companion. Stelle quickly became accustomed to the sweet conversation. Ava was kind, lively and showed excitement for the smallest everyday occurrence. It was pleasant to be around someone so content with their simple life, and despite the difference in rank, Stelle would miss her when she left the Lark. They sat together on the balcony watching the retrieval of various items, walked up and down the halls, and shared meals. It was what she imagined friendship with her sisters should have been, had they been born into a different life. It was what she shared with Lucy in moments when no one was watching. It was probably similar to the friendship Lucy and Wynter had shared, a friendship Stelle knew she couldn't be a part of. The memory stung a little, but here on the Lark there was a sense of freedom in her comportment that she hadn't experienced before.

If it wasn't Ava with her, Merrick was by her side. Stelle had the sneaking suspicion she was being watched at all times and often directed away from certain areas of the Lark.

Amusing. As if she cared what secrets lay beyond the closed doors of a salvage ship.

Her little adventure would be quite a story to tell. Stelle let a bit of pride settle neatly into her heart. She'd dined with crew, talked to pilots, and survived the ordinary dresses.

Stelle knew she wouldn't be the same person upon her return; an adventure like this must have truly changed her. Spending time with the common crew was a strange novelty that was coming to an end. They should be nearing the midway station, even if the Lark was a slower-moving ship.

In her room, she gathered her few belongings to prepare for their imminent arrival. Finding only one shoe, she lifted blankets and pillows and pushed around the general mess. She spied the sparkled heel under a white sheet. Swiping it toward her, she caught the edge of a discarded dress. Ava had found a dozen dresses for her, but they had all been simple and fit poorly.

Stelle had planned to remake this one but had forgotten once it was under her bed. The bright orange and yellow swirls on the silk reminded her of a sunburst. Running the fabric through her fingers, she decided she wanted to leave the Lark in a style befitting a lady.

With black scissors in hand, she set the open blades to the red pleated silk, then slid them up in a wobbled, uneven line. Creating a ribbon effect, she layered the streams of ribbon over an off-white skirt. Slicing a long ribbon off another skirt, she tied it over the top, hiding the uneven stitches and cinching it in at her waist. The bottom was tied, showing the barest hint of skin. A sash swept over her shoulder and draped down. Stelle inspected her appearance in the narrow mirror. Satisfied, she adorned her neck with the thick string of diamonds.

Dancing into the hall, Stelle twirled and let the ribboned skirt have a full swish, the edges tickling the walls. It was another accomplishment she knew she would have to tell Lucy about.

One final twirl, and the hall felt like it was narrowing. The door ahead of her spun. Her foot took a misstep to the side, and she braced herself against the wall. Or rather, the ship shifted under her feet.

She knew they must be close to docking, but there would have been an announcement if they were going to stop.

Stelle put her hand on the wall and sensed the movement of the ship.

This didn't feel like stopping.

The pilots would have to be amateurs to rock the entire ship, and in the brief time she'd spent with Sers and Lavalle, she could tell they weren't the type to make a mistake.

One foot in front of the other, she felt it again.

Like a pull against the hull, it was almost as if they were entering an orbit—like a landing shuttle. But a craft like this surely stayed in space.

Panic clawed at the edges of her mind.

Another unmistakable sway hit the ship. Stelle's fingers curled around the diamonds that pressed against her throat. Forcing herself to breathe, panic gripped her.

Like the Monrovia, the Lark was going to pull apart.

Where were the alarms?

No one was in the halls. Could they already be in a safety shuttle? Had they left her behind? Merrick hadn't shown her where the emergency access was.

She could either run to the control room or make her way to her own safety pod.

Sprinting, Stelle let the ribbons fly behind her as she raced toward the pod. Then she felt it again—the shift of the ship rattle.

Locked doors barred her entrance to the salvage area. She couldn't open them. Banging on the lights, she cried into the small comm.

She couldn't do this again. Her fist banged the security lock again and again until the alarm tripped and sirens sounded through the ship. The blaring sound sunk into her skull.

She closed her eyes and bunched the ribbons of her skirt in her hand. The delicate fabrics were fraying at the rough cut edges and bits of thread fluttered from her hands to the floor. A scream tried to crawl from her lungs, but there wasn't any air. Somehow, the hull had already been breached.

It was too late; the air was already depleted from the hallway. Her chest ached. How did it happen so fast? Blackness inched around the edge of her eyes. She squeezed them tight. Her heart hammered like it was going to explode. The Monrovia had happened fast; she'd barely had time to think. Now every second lasted an eternity as her lungs used up their remaining oxygen.

Voices blared with the sound of the alarms she had set off. There was someone else in the hall with her. They hadn't all abandoned her to the safety pod.

Frail arms reached out to Stelle, and she felt as though she would break them if she held on any tighter.

Eyes still closed, someone shifted her Merrick. She knew it was him. He smelled like rain on the Valtine lavender fields.

Home—she wanted to be home before she died.

"She's going to pass out," Jasper said from somewhere down the hall as they lowered her body to the floor.

Panic gripped her again. They couldn't sit on the floor—they needed to move fast to get to safety.

Pushing against her rescuer, the Lark rock again and heard herself let out a pathetic whimper.

"It's only flares. They happen out here all the time." Merrick's voice broke through the fog in her mind. He was clear and logical, but soft. "Try to breathe slowly. I'm touching your hand. Can you feel my hand?"

His fingers traced the inside of her palm; awareness shot like lightning through her. She was leaning against Merrick, who was leaning against a wall. His well-muscled arms were holding her. Embarrassment crept up from her toes to her fingertips.

He was talking in a low, infuriatingly smooth voice. Not as if she were a child, but as if he'd done this before. There was oxygen, and she was breathing. They all were.

Getting her bearings, she pushed away from him a little.

"What was that?" Stelle asked.

"Only the flares. Sorry, I didn't even think to mention them," Merrick apologized.

"*The flares*? What are those? What do you mean they happen out here? We should be at the midway station."

He let go of her hand but didn't answer her.

She pushed away from him and stood up on shaking legs, still trying to get regular gulps of air. Standing with her, he tried to reach out and steady her arm, but she flung him away.

Her anxiety was being replaced with anger and something deeper.

They weren't going back to the midway station.

"Where are we?" Stelle asked.

No one said anything for a moment. Ava's hands were over her mouth, eyes wide. Jasper was leaning against the wall, knife flicking.

"We're passing through some rough areas toward Tornillo. There are going to be flares and occasional debris depending on the route we take. We'll stop and get you going in the right direction as soon as we can, but flares are going to happen," Merrick said.

"No—No—No." Stelle pushed him hard in the chest. He looked down at her as another flare rocked them towards each other.

Grabbing his arms, she clung on, despite her anger, and tried to stop her hands from shaking. The scent of lavender rain hit her again. She latched onto the scent and breathed it in, waiting for her heart to stop hammering.

"You will turn this ship around and take me home," Stelle said, tears pricking at the edge of her eyes.

"No—I will not."

Nine

Merrick saw the terror in her eyes. Like the ship was being ripped apart all over again. He knew what it was like to push all of those feelings down, bury them, hide them, only to have them come out at the worst possible moment.

He had been planning on telling her they were heading to Tornillo, but since he hadn't decided what to do with her once they got there, he had waited to reveal their destination. In hindsight, that was not the best idea.

The pulses from nearby stars were harmless to the Lark but unsettling, which is why few ships took this quicker route.

Stelle stormed down the hall. The red streamers were like heralds of flame as they licked around her swishing hips. Merrick followed quickly behind and almost caught up when she broke all semblance of being a lady and sprinted away. She was heading to the bridge where Sers and Lavalle were monitoring their progress through the flares, making sure the ship didn't skim too close to the bursts.

Stelle slowed, squared her shoulders and walked into the room as if she were wearing a crown and not a home-made disaster.

Stealing up beside Sers, Stelle put one hand on her hip and the other she motioned at the pilots.

"This ship will turn around immediately," she declared, obviously convinced they would obey her command.

Merrick stood in the doorway, waiting to step in only if needed. He was almost a little sorry for Stelle.

"What's this commotion on my bridge?" Sers said, swivelling his chair to take Stelle in. "Hey Lavalle, looks like Merrick's got himself a firebug." He stretched his legs long and leaned back with his hands behind his head.

"You know what, Sers," Lavalle started, his face focused forward, twitching his upper lip, making the thick moustache dance. "I bet she's riled up because of something Jasper said. They probably didn't even throw a welcoming dinner for the lady, and you know who ends up taking her tanking attitude?"

"Us," Sers said.

"That's right—*us*." Lavalle flicked up a dial. It probably didn't need checking. There wasn't much to do at this point but monitor things, but Lavalle always tried to look busy.

"We're just pilots, you know. Been doing this for longer than they've been breathing. And this is the thanks we get," Sers said, turning back to the screens, obviously dismissing Stelle.

"We didn't get any welcome dinner."

"That's cause we were here before them," Sers reminded him.

"You know, the last captain… now he was a useless fellow… he'd throw dinners for us and make sure we were invited."

Stelle looked from one to the other, lips pursed, and took a shallow breath.

"You will turn this ship around." Her voice raised in pitch. Sers and Lavalle wouldn't touch the navigation; not without clearing it with Merrick.

"Two more to go," Lavalle said to Sers, who nodded and focused on the screens in front of them.

"Two more? Ten more because you're going to turn this ship—" Stelle started. But the ship gently rocked, exactly like it should to absorb the impact without throwing anything off. Merrick stepped forward and put his hand under Stelle's elbow for a moment. She didn't seem to notice it as she breathed in sharply.

Jasper noticed as he joined them on the bridge. He glowered at Merrick, who shrugged and stepped back once the ship stilled.

"How long do you think you can keep me here without someone noticing? The whole galaxy is going to be looking for me," Stelle said.

Merrick closed his eyes, accepting again his failure to communicate. Sers didn't say a word, but passed Stelle a datapad with the list of the casualties from the Monrovia.

"Maybe it would be best if we turned around," Ava said softly as she joined them. She looped her thin arm through Merrick's.

Merrick looked down at her, waiting for Stelle to process the new information "That's not going to happen."

"We might not make it in time, anyway," Ava said softly.

That was a punch to the gut. The trip was his plan. It was dangerous and reckless to venture this far with Ava.

"If it were only that, it would be enough for me to stay the course. But by turning around, we would draw a lot of attention." He tried to sound convincing. This was the first bit of hope they'd enjoyed, and he would not let it go.

"But she's a lady… a genuine lady," Ava whispered.

"No titles on the Lark," Merrick said.

Ava nodded, then turned to Stelle. "It's hard to be out this far. I can't imagine doing it without planning for it."

"Final one," Lavalle called to the uninterested room.

The ship rocked Stelle close again. She placed a hand against Merrick's chest to keep from leaning into him.

"Every second I am on this ship, I will make you regret not turning around the moment I boarded. When you found out who I was, you should have thought twice before carrying on with your pathetic salvage mission."

She pushed off and like a beacon ablaze, strode down the hall.

Ten

For the next few days, Stelle tried everything to make Merrick turn the ship around. Her societal influence was clearly yielding no results, so she resorted to the futile task of wearing him down.

He didn't mind her following him, humming and singing. She sat in his workroom, dumping the pile from the chair onto the floor. He didn't even look up.

Stelle talked endlessly about balls and parties. Many of the stories involved the lengths required to keep her sister out of trouble, in which Stelle often created a scene to divert the attention away from her. Lady Violet couldn't handle the censure of Valtine, while Stelle thrived off the gossip. She talked about Lord Kent and how he genuinely disapproved of everything she did—unlike the way she pretended to disapprove of everyone else. She told him about the Obsidian and how Helix, a fashion designer, was actually a fraud.

He nodded and occasionally looked up, crossing his arms to appear as if he was listening, but would return back to his work without comment.

As the stories were proving more a source of entertainment than annoyance, she absconded with a few of his wires, tucking them into the folds of her skirt. She liked the way he ran his hand over his unshaved jawline, as he looked for them. But soon he pulled another box of wires out from under a pile of silver tubes, replacing what he needed.

The following day, Stelle took the wires out of her pocket and braided them together into a tiny ring. She couldn't get it to stay joined. Merrick looked up for a moment, took the almost-ring out of her hands, and made a tiny arc, welding the ends together and passing it back.

Stelle stared at the ring in her palm. When she didn't put it on, he passed her a weightless chain and wire cutters. She cut herself a length and hung it around her neck.

It only took four days before Stelle gave up and decided to try bothering the copilots.

Sers and Lavalle were equally relaxed about her presence and constant demands. She tried to get a rise out of them, but anytime she entered the bridge, they would outmatch her ability to talk. Lavalle would cluck over something Jasper said; or Sers would crow about all the things he professed to know about the Lark, space travel, datapad links for communication, and on and on.

Stewing, Stelle changed tactics. If she couldn't bully or annoy them, she would be sweet and persuade them. Stelle spent a full two hours carefully weaving every single strand of her hair into perfectly placed coils. Then the following morning, she unravelled the plaits and let them hang crimped to perfection. She slid an armory of cold jewelled rings onto her fingers to add a little sparkle, and wore the braided ring around her neck.

When she reached the lounge, everyone was busy. Ruse and Ava were playing a game at the side table. A square checkerboard was between them, with rows of flat round discs lined up on either side. She watched for a minute as each disc flipped from black to white, then back again.

On the other side of the table, Merrick was deep in conversation with Jasper. A mound of wires and a control board the size of a small plate sat piled in front of them.

Jasper glared, pulled the ridiculous knife out of his pocket, and spun it around, blades out, between his fingers. There was something about him that reminded Stelle of Valtine; maybe it was his condescending manner.

Stelle sashayed past them, as if she hadn't planned on looking at the datapads, and found herself at the counter, feeling uncomfortable.

"Ava, would you like me to make you some tea?" Stelle asked as calmly as she could.

Ava's eyes grew wide. She looked at Merrick, then Jasper.

"Oh, umm, yes, tea would be lovely," Ava said kindly.

Stelle took a deep breath. Making tea couldn't be difficult. Typically, Ava preferred the mug with little blue flowers. Ruse always used the black one with a stone-looking finish. Jasper just grabbed the one closest to the front, and Merrick used a jade-green mug and offered her the matching one when it was available.

She picked the mugs for Ava and herself. Setting them on the counter, she looked into the bottoms and then at the kettle that may as well have grown teeth.

The kettle was shiny and smooth. Several opal-topped brass

buttons lined the edge like the valves of a French horn. Lifting the kettle, she heard a small slosh at the bottom. It needed more water but wouldn't open. The button on the side didn't release the top, and pulling up on it wasn't working either.

A startled yelp escaped her lips when Merrick came up behind her.

He cleared his throat. "Let me show you how. I designed this one myself, so it won't be what you're likely used to."

They both knew she had never held a kettle before, but with the daggers Jasper was sending her way, she was thankful for the lie. His arm brushed against hers, and she stepped to the side, only to bump into him again as he reached around to fill the kettle. Stelle felt like she was at a dance but didn't know the moves.

He held the handle down, filled it, and clipped it into the bracket on the wall. It held to the base and released when it was hot.

Merrick pulled out a little drawer with a variety of teas and jars. She picked a few she thought would blend well, careful to not bump into him again.

Stelle poured the tea into mugs for herself and Ava, while Merrick reached over her shoulder to get mugs for himself and Jasper.

She passed the cup to Ava, smiling triumphantly.

"Learning a new trick doesn't make you one of us," Jasper said from the table. He was holding a datapad for Merrick to inspect and appeared annoyed by the delay she had caused.

"Oh, come off it, Jasper. You of all people—" Ava started but was cut off by Ruse.

"We're all stuck here together. Might as well make the best

of it," Ruse smiled, showing a row of teeth and flipping two of the discs over.

"What is it that you all have against titles? It's a little hypocritical, don't you think?" She stood near the table, watching the game unfold. "Even on a ship this small, there's an order. Like it or not, you all take orders from *Captain* Merrick. If it was any other way, I'd be home by now."

Jasper was fuming, and Stelle expected to see his irritating knife flick out.

"Merrick's worth listening to. He was given the title of Captain because he earned it. This crew doesn't follow him blindly because of some unnatural genetic coding our ancestors added to our DNA. You've probably never earned anything in your entire spoiled life."

"Earning the title of Captain of a salvage ship is quite the achievement. I'm happy to hear you've earned the place beneath him." The sarcasm rolled off her tongue as second nature. She hated the cutting words and the bitterness that welled up inside, but she couldn't stop herself. It was the only way to control things in her world. How many times had she not been able to stop every acidic thought from coming out?

She was spoiled. With her wealth, it was impossible not to be lavished with every comfort. But Jasper was wrong. Everything she did was for someone else. She protected her sister, lied for Lady Daye, and defended her friends. It was useless arguing with someone as thick as Jasper. He'd made a decision about her without even knowing her, and there was nothing wrong with wanting to go home. Instead of countering him, she focused on the board in front of her.

"Teach me this game," Stelle demanded, motioning for

Ruse to get up from his seat. Ruse pushed his chair back and stood, allowing her to take his seat. Ava took a sip of her tea and started resetting the board as the tension in the room eased.

"It's so simple, but there are some rules you need to know. You're black, and you're trying to take over my white. As long as one of us has at least one disc left, the game isn't over," Ava explained.

"So how do I make yours turn black?" Stelle asked. The game sounded simple enough.

"You can choose a variety of moves. I'll explain as we go."

They spent the next few minutes moving pieces forward. Ava informed Stelle when she needed to flip hers over, and it appeared to be a simple enough game.

"Wait. Why did you put the one back there back to white?" Stelle asked.

"Because you reached the end with your black—you can't do that."

"I didn't know that." Stelle focused on the discs, wondering how she missed the rule.

"Are you sure? I thought I mentioned it," Ava said, giving her a wide-eyed, genuine look of surprise.

Stelle looked at the board. She was clearly winning until Ava put a previously removed white one back on.

"You have four in a row. See? Which means I get to take one as mine," Ava said triumphantly.

"I can't have four in a row?" Stelle gasped. Her apparent victory was quickly falling apart.

"It's a simple game. Are you having trouble?" Merrick leaned over her shoulder. His nearness sent a tingle up her spine as he put his hand on the back of her chair.

"If you move this one here, you can take hers—see?" He pointed to two pieces. Stelle didn't see, but she couldn't admit that she had failed to keep up with the rules.

Jasper also took an interest in the game. The entire group was now watching her intently.

She wished she were wearing a fancy ball gown, something dazzling and distracting. Something to keep them from focusing on her.

Stelle wasn't particularly competitive, but she needed to prove something. She needed to win this.

Eleven

Merrick looked down at Stelle. A cute furrow had crossed her brow as she concentrated on the board in front of her. She hadn't picked up on Ava's joke and was taking the game rather seriously.

"You think I should put this there?" Stelle asked. She tilted her chin up slightly and looked him in the eye. Perhaps she was more perceptive than he'd thought.

"I really do," Merrick said, his voice low in her ear, offering no other explanation for the move.

Stelle hesitated, then moved the piece.

Ava smiled in triumph. It was good to see Ava so animated and enjoying herself. He caught a glimpse of what the future might have been for her, and his heart constricted. It was moments like this that kept him pushing the Lark.

"Wait, what did I do? What's wrong?" Stelle cried. Merrick tried not to laugh. Jasper was already chuckling.

"Merrick, you forgot the primary rule," Ava taunted. "Sorry, Stelle—if you have one in each corner, the game is lost!"

"Wait … what? I didn't know. I lost? But I have almost all black on the board. I should be allowed to take it back—Merrick suggested it. I wasn't even going to play there!" Stelle looked as though she wanted to throw the board. Even upset, she looked like a lady. The way she tilted her head and pressed her lips together set her apart.

Jasper's shoulders were shaking, and Ava scrunched her face, her chin quivering.

"That's not how you play the game at all, is it?" Stelle asked.

"I'm sorry, but after the past few days it was our turn," Ava blurted out, shaking with laughter. There was something soft and silvery about Ava's laughter. Even Jasper seemed to be affected by the sound.

Stelle tried to push the chair back, but it bumped Merrick's legs. He placed his hands on top of her shoulders and applied a light pressure, squeezing them.

"Take it as a compliment. Ava only tricks people she considers part of the crew," he said. Stelle shook her shoulders, and he released his hold on them. A wave of ice come off her, and he realized she wasn't taking it well.

Jasper was still chuckling. Stelle turned and faced him and glared at the datapad he'd been shielding her from.

"I might not be good at a child's game, but I can't imagine you are good at anything. I still haven't figured out exactly what it is you do around here," Stelle said, glaring at the illuminated piece of tech.

"What I do is none of your concern," Jasper replied, pushing his screen out of sight but directly into the line of Ava's view. Jasper's temporarily good mood vanished and with it,

Merrick's enjoyment of the moment.

"Come to think of it, I don't know what Ava does around here either," Stelle said.

"Ava?" Jasper asked absently, only partially committed to the conversation.

Merrick looked over at her, wanting to stop whatever she was going to say next.

"Ava doesn't cook or clean, and yet you all seem careful to bring her tea and whatever else she wants…"

"Careful, Stelle." The warning came from Jasper. The rest of the room got very still. Stelle ignored him, apparently unable to hold back her tirade.

"Clearly, she's only here to keep someone *company*. I have no intention of lowering myself to join the ranks of this ship if you think that's why you wanted to keep me around—" The sound of a chair scraping on the floor stopped her. Merrick was angry. It was the first time Stelle had truly upset him, and the crew knew it. After the kindness Ava had shown Stelle, she shouldn't have said that.

Jasper picked the datapads up off the table without even looking in her direction and left. Ruse followed, his expression unreadable. Ava was the last to get up, gathering her things. The full cups of tea were abandoned on the table.

Ava placed a hand on Merrick's arm.

"Captain," she said, almost in a whisper. "It's okay."

It wasn't okay. Ava had been happy, playing a joke. Stelle had been cruel, and he didn't know what to say to her. Jasper had been warning him that Stelle was pretending to play commoner, and that it would end badly. Ruse had made numerous comments over the past few days regarding the wrongness of having a lady on board.

Stelle picked up two of the mugs off of the table and dumped the contents down the kitchen sink. Merrick followed her movements, waiting for her to say something else. Instead, she pulled the kettle off the wall, fumbling to remove the lid.

Merrick finally moved in close behind. Turning to face him, she held the kettle for him to open. He took it from her, then reached around to set it on the counter.

"She called you Captain. I thought you didn't use titles on the ship." Her words came out cold. Merrick weighed what he wanted to say in return.

"You can say whatever you want to me. I don't mind. It's my fault you're here and not home already," he started.

Stelle rolled her eyes.

"But Stelle," he paused, wanting to be clear, finding the dagger in the silence. "You don't get to talk about Ava like that."

He was toe to toe with her, looking down as she backed against the counter and grasped the edge behind her.

"You can call me Stelle all you want, but my name is Lady Cristelle, and I know exactly who I am. You can't tell me what to do or what not to do. I can't control how people react to the things I say. It's not my problem if she took offence."

"You're going to apologize to her," he stated, not taking her bait.

"Or what?" Stelle said. "You're going to lock me in some closet for the rest of the trip? Starve me? Take away my tea privileges? You can't force me to say sorry. Do your worst." Her voice shook, and for a moment, she looked afraid.

He took a step back, his voice low. "No, Stelle—no. No one

here would do anything to hurt you."

"Then why threaten me?" She glared back. He could see the tears that threatened to spill over.

"It wasn't a threat. I told you because it's what you need to do—to reconsider—because Ava doesn't deserve your ill treatment. It's the right thing to do."

"I don't need your approval."

"No, you don't need my approval. But you should at least want your own." Merrick let the words fall between them.

* * *

Merrick hid on the bridge and half listened to Jasper argue with Lavalle about docking, wishing he could go back and say something else to Stelle.

Insulting Ava had been childish and cruel, but Stelle had been thrust into a world unknown to her. The past few days she'd told him story after story about her life, and he was quickly putting together a picture of a Valtine lady who manipulated and destroyed those around her when she was backed into a corner. She cared very little about her own image and was more concerned with breaking her mother's rules than with what people thought of her. And at the end of each story, it was most often revealed that her actions were meant for the protection of others. It was a sentiment he could sympathize with.

He knew her choice of dresses was far inferior to what she was used to, but she managed to make the most of everything in the trunks and somehow still look exceptional. The butter-yellow flowers on her dress today were soft and flowy. He did his best to not notice how the gown hugged her curves and fell to the floor. She looked stunning.

"She's not like the others," Jasper said. "You can't rescue her."

"She doesn't need to be rescued," Merrick replied and took the offered datapad out of Lavalle's hand.

Stelle *wasn't* like the others, and she would be heading home soon, which is what they were discussing. It was the next problem that needed to be solved, even if all of the options were less than favourable. Transferring her to one of their other ships on Tornillo was the best option. Lavalle had contacts he could reach out to, people who would bring her home to Valtine.

"Let's focus on the job, and Lavalle can arrange transport for Stelle back home," Merrick said.

"I already arranged transport for Stelle. Lex said—for the right price—he could skip a full docking on Tornillo, and reroute his recent coordinates to appear like he'd been scavenging closer to Valtine."

"Why didn't you say something?" Merrick asked.

"You look like you need a place to hide," Sers said.

"I'm not hiding," Merrick mumbled.

Ava joined them on the bridge, hands on her hips. Even in her frailty, she looked formidable. "What are you doing here?"

"We're busy—busy, busy, busy," Lavalle murmured, taking a sip of tea. A full plate of round puffy biscuits balanced on his knees.

"I'm flying the ship," Sers said.

"The ship flies itself," Ava retorted. "You two don't need to be here unless one of your little alarms goes off, and they give you ample notice. I meant him." She pointed at Merrick.

"Me? Where else would I be?"

"With Stelle! Did you tell her? Oh, you didn't say anything, did you? You probably only made her feel bad, and now you're what? Planning how to get her off the ship? She's not a problem; she's a person."

"She doesn't know how to be a person," Jasper said, not making eye contact with Ava, who turned to glare at him too.

"If you're too scared to be kind to a lady, then I will. Where is she?!" Ava boomed.

"Trying to get into where we have the safety pod stored. One of my little alarms is going off." Lavalle pointed to the blinking light.

"Then let her in," Ava demanded.

"That's a restricted area." Merrick's brow creased. He felt as though a tiny tornado had whipped through his non-hiding place.

"And let me in when I get down there! Seriously! You are lucky you have me on the ship." Ava fled, leaving the men to stare after her. At Merrick's nod Lavalle released the lock to the clearance doors, allowing access to the safety pod.

Jasper glowered.

"How much will Ava tell her?" Jasper asked, clearly not liking the situation.

"It's Ava. She won't tell her anything. She'll leave it to me."

"You sure?" Jasper asked.

"No," Merrick said. Ava had expected him to tell Stelle about the Lark, and it hadn't even crossed his mind. She'd be leaving soon—the less she knew, the better.

Twelve

Stelle stomped her feet as she made her way to the cargo hold. She tried to ignore the stray bit of moisture that pooled under her lashes and fell down her cheek.

It wasn't new. Lady Lucy was the only one who ever stuck around, and Stelle had been terrible the last time she'd seen her. Stelle had been jealous of her new friendship and had let Lucy steal a dress for Wynter. But instead of looking terrible in the dress as Stelle had hoped, Wynter had looked lovely.

Letting the memory swirl into the mess of her current emotions, Stelle reached the level where her escape pod was stored. The containment unit apparently worked both ways. She couldn't get out when she first arrived, and now she couldn't enter. She mashed the numbered buttons on the control panel until a little whirl of lights went off.

Stelle looked down at the pod, waiting. She wanted to crawl into it, to let it shoot her back into space. Leaning her head against the wall, she fought to control her emotions.

The sound of the door opening surprised her, but she didn't turn to see who it was. She didn't care who had opened it.

The door to her pod was sideways on the floor, wires and parts hanging out of it. She carefully stepped over the wreck, wishing she could fix it, go back in time, and start the whole adventure over again.

There was a familiar tug in her heart. The pod was lonely. It was hollow, small, and it still smelled faintly of perfume.

The second containment door swished open, announcing an intruder.

"Hi Stelle," Ava said, as if it were the most natural thing to be standing in a torn-apart safety pod.

"You don't have to come and pretend to be my friend anymore. I've officially proven I am incapable of having one of those. Don't feel sorry for me. I don't mind at all. People like me are only fit for society with other people like me," Stelle said, all in one breath.

"Oh, well. That's dark. I came down here because Jasper doesn't want anyone in this room, and I thought it would be funny to make him stress."

Stelle let out a short laugh. "Someone let me in."

"Lavalle… I told him to, and Merrick didn't stop him."

"He probably hopes I'll hit something and suck myself out of the airlock."

"Maybe."

The whole thing was so terrible, and Ava was giggling.

"It's not funny, Ava," Stelle said.

"It kind of is," Ava said, between breaths.

Stelle considered the past hour: the way Ava had played the game prank, her own horrible reaction and insecurity. Involuntarily, Stelle was laughing too, but it was full of sadness and relief and frustration at herself and everyone else. This whole situation was so ridiculous.

Stelle sank to the floor and kicked a little pile of rubble.

Ava sat beside her, knees tucked up against her chest. They settled in and so did the reality of where they were.

"It's tiny in here," Ava said, in barely a whisper. Even with the side panel open, it was small. The smell of stale flux gases still clung to the sterile environment.

"I think *they* knew I was out there, in the safety pod. I think they knew they were leaving me behind." Stelle looked at the floor, at the bits. Copper-toned wires curled around silver tubes embedded with iridescent chips. Merrick said the parts were worth more all scattered and torn up. Stelle would have thought an intact ship would have more value, but salvage often supplied what someone else needed. Pulling at one of the exposed wires, she yanked on it until it dislodged from the interior of the hull.

"I'm sure that's not what happened," Ava said, picking up her own bit of wire to fiddle with. "Besides, Merrick said the sensors were all wonky."

Merrick said the sensors were wonky? He hadn't informed her. If there was a malfunction with the sensors, then no one would have picked her up—ever. No one would have been looking for her.

"If Merrick hadn't…" Stelle choked off the words. Silence danced around the pod, giving Stelle a few minutes to collect herself.

"I like your hair—how long did it take?" Ava asked. Stelle ran her hands over the perfect wave of dark brown hair. Not even a wisp was out of place.

Stelle stood and motioned for Ava to sit in the chair, the

chair that had carried her for days. "Here, sit in front of me, and I can do yours in braids. It doesn't take long."

"My sister liked braiding my hair, but she was terrible at it. Got it all in knots or a puffy mess," Ava said, and flopped onto the chair in front of Stelle.

"My sisters are all younger, and would never sit still long enough for me to do their hair. Violet has blonde hair like yours but with big thick curls—and I'm sorry I said those things about you."

The apology was hurried, tacked onto the end. The words were unnatural. Like they belonged to someone else, someone she wished she could be.

Ava smiled. "It's okay. I think Merrick was more upset than anyone. He can get protective. Especially after Helen died."

"Was Helen your sister?" Stelle asked.

"No, my sister's name was Chrysanthemum. She's been gone for a while. Helen was just a friend on the Lark with us."

Stelle stared down at her dress, wondering if it was Helen's clothing she was wearing.

Stelle pulled the pieces of Ava's hair back and worked the strands together into a long braid, the repetition calming her nerves.

"She was cozy with Ruse. That flower dress was one of her favourites, and you look so lovely in it. She would have laughed to have seen it on a real lady." Ava folded her hands in her lap, her frail shoulders hunched over.

Stelle stopped braiding for a moment, the wispy strands hanging limp between her fingers. She couldn't imagine knowing so much loss at such a young age.

"Laughed? None of you know how to get angry properly.

You should all be enraged that someone is wearing your friend's gowns," Stelle said, looking down at what she was wearing, a little angry at herself. In Valtine, she never asked permission for anything, but now she wished she had.

"No one is angry at you, especially not Merrick. I think he was disappointed because he likes you."

"We come from different worlds," Stelle said swiftly, wondering why she hadn't outright denied it. She worked with Ava's hair until the braid curled into a pretty coil.

"You're two sides of the same coin. Merrick fixes everything by holding it inside—like a white hot fire, close to his chest, where no one can touch it. With you, I think you try to fix things by making everyone around you dark. If you can spread the dark, then it lessens your own pain. Both untouchable. I don't envy either of you."

Stelle stiffened. She didn't like being told that she was bringing darkness to others, but Ava understood her in a way no one else had ever tried to.

Her childhood had been perfect. Expert tutors taught her exactly how to manage the vast properties she would one day inherit. Etiquette and rules proved essential once she began to mingle in society, no matter how harsh the road to learning them. Everything was always gowns, parties, dinners, and lessons. It would be wrong to complain. And she knew it was worse for her sister who struggled to find her way.

Stelle wondered if her family would close up the house on Valtine when they got news of the Monrovia. Stelle knew no one was looking for her. In the highest ranks of Valtine court, life had to continue after death. All the rules of Idex and waiting ten years without a body didn't apply to them. They would pay someone to make the necessary changes—they had probably already forgotten her.

"I don't have any pain. My life is pleasant. How do you handle problems, since you're such an expert?" Stelle knew she was getting defensive and proving Ava right. She looked at the fruit bar she had kicked under the desk, now covered with bits of wire, and wondered why Ava thought Merrick carried pain.

"Chrysanthemum would say: you need to let someone love you," Ava said. She sounded like Lucy, sweet and sheltered.

Ava stood and, in a blink, wrapped her arms around Stelle.

Thin arms squeezed tighter as Stelle tried to pull back; the scent of flowers and tea clung to her.

Stelle relaxed a little, wondering when the hug was going to end. She blocked the part out of her mind where something was trying to sneak in. Break in. She pushed it aside; she couldn't allow it. It would hurt too much.

Stelle could have pried Ava's arms apart, but she didn't. And Ava didn't let go. It was as if Ava was trying to squeeze the memories from her, to share them with her.

She wasn't sure when she started crying—not big gushing tears—but small ones that had been sitting, waiting for days to come out.

When Ava pulled away, Stelle wiped them with the back of her sleeve and pretended like they hadn't fallen.

"I think I have something sparkly to add to your hair," Stelle said, leaving the safety pod. She led Ava from the room and joked how the rest of the crew would be relieved to have it locked up tight again.

She rushed down the hall to find a pin for Ava's hair.

Something had changed, altered.

Stelle didn't like the feeling; a bit of herself was missing, exposed, and open. She wanted to close it up. But attempting to push the feeling away only sparked new tears. The harder she tried to stuff the feeling in, the more the edges around the wall crumbled.

Ava had forgiven her and received nothing in return; and what was worse, Stelle had barely apologized. The need to find a pin for Ava's hair grew, as did the need to get out of the dead woman's dress.

Thirteen

Ava's scream tore through the Lark.

They were three days from Tornillo. Merrick was in his shop, working endlessly on Stelle's safety pod, trying to provide her with answers before they parted ways. As far as plans went, it was as good as they could hope for. Stelle had agreed to say nothing about the Lark and claim it had all been a grand adventure. She'd just been waiting to see the look on everyone's faces when she made it back to Valtine.

Ava's static call for help crackled through the ship's comms again. Merrick made a mental note to fix the communication lines, then abandoned his work on Stelle's safety pod and rushed to the dining room.

Ava was standing at the door waiting for him, tears streaming down her cheeks.

Merrick brushed past her. Stelle was reclining on the chaise, skirts fanned in a perfect arc of deep-green day dress. Her toe poked out of the bottom and her head tilted back, eyes open.

Jasper was kneeling down beside her, checking for a pulse. Sers and Lavalle were shuffling through the room, picking up random items, then tossing them back down.

Lavalle picked up a teacup. He brought it up to his nose and inhaled deeply, then pushed Jasper out of the way.

"We need the doctor," Ava cried, grabbing onto Merrick's arm. Her fingers pressed in, leaving half-moon nail marks. "Why isn't he here?"

"No time to get the doctor—Sers, grab me a lionium kit," Lavalle said. He pulled at the ruffled sleeve on Stelle's dress while Sers located the med kit from the bottom drawer.

Sers unhinged the case, and the sound of the metal clips popping rang through the galley. He dumped it on the floor, then tossed Lavalle a syringe.

Without hesitation, Lavalle stuck Stelle in the arm.

Lavalle leaned back on his hands, giving Jasper room to push his way back in.

"What happened?" Merrick asked Ava. Ava blew her nose and dabbed at her tears.

"I don't know. I came in and Stelle was reading—well, she had a book in her lap. I sat down beside her, and—and her eyes rolled into her head, and she just collapsed. Shouldn't we call the doctor?" Ava whispered the question.

"She'll be fine. Why don't you help Sers with whatever he's doing?" Merrick suggested. Ava reluctantly joined Sers in the kitchen giving Merrick room. He watched as Jasper focused on Stelle's breathing.

"I was working on Stelle's safety pod," Merrick said quietly, trying to figure out the data he'd compiled while he sat helplessly waiting for Stelle to wake up.

"The blast pattern on the side of the pod shows it was released before the major explosion; maybe it even caused it. If they didn't make the cloaking technology compatible with the rest of the Monrovia—it could have caused a failure in safety measures. The blowback from the thrusters could have triggered a chain reaction through the lower part of the Monrovia. It's just a theory, and it has lots of holes, but until I can get a schematic of the explosion, I won't likely find the truth."

He wouldn't be able to tell Stelle why she was left in space, and they might never know.

Merrick was thankful for one thing. The technology used was not as detailed as he thought. It showed signs of hasty construction, and although it evaded regular scans, its capabilities ended there.

"Found it!" Sers called from the kitchen. Merrick joined Ava and Sers as they assessed the containers on the table. He rubbed his jaw.

"This here is a medicinal tea—it's to balance the long effects of flux gas exposure if you don't have an anti-serum handy. And this is for Corva-cold. Mixed, they create lionium poison," Sers explained, holding up the jars of mixed leaves. They looked like tea, but not like any of the blends they'd used lately.

"How do you know that?" Merrick asked.

"What you want to know is what they were doing in the kitchen. These herbs need to be stored in sealed containers, not on a tea trolly." Sers put the small jars into the medical case and sealed the latches.

"Wait, Sers found the tea after you stuck her with the syringe! You might have killed her," Ava said, wagging the syringe in the air.

"She was already dead—it wouldn't have made a

difference," Lavalle defended himself. "I was fairly certain."

Stelle moved in her seat and mumbled while chatter flew around the room.

Jasper made a comment about the dangers of teaching ladies to make tea. Ava kept asking why no one had bothered to get the doctor. Lavalle was giving a lecture about the proper storage of medicinal teas and all the worst case scenarios from not following the directions closely.

"I don't feel well," Stelle said, putting a delicate hand over her forehead. Her breathing was shallow, but there was colour in her cheeks. Merrick retrieved a cold compress from the icebox and brought it over to her.

"You mixed some brew," Sers said before taking the empty syringe from Ava and putting it into the bin. "You almost died."

"I don't remember doing that," Stelle murmured, leaning back and pressing the cold compress into her face. "And I'm already dead."

Merrick grimaced at her attempted joke. Sers and Lavalle were smiling, perhaps at Stelle's recovery, or perhaps because they'd been the ones to bring it about. Ava was teary-eyed. Even Jasper looked relieved. It appeared to be an accident; still something was wrong about the whole situation. Merrick just couldn't place what it was.

Fourteen

A gloom had settled over the Lark. Two days until Tornillo.

Stelle started drinking coffee instead of tea. Merrick roasted it perfectly for her, even though he never drank any. Stelle sat with a teacup in her hand at the far end of the long room, watching the steam curl and vanish.

Jasper and Merrick were over in the kitchen, talking with Ruse at the table. The confidential datapads passed between the crew, and hushed plans made her want to roll her eyes. Whatever they were involved in, it didn't even matter in the world she belonged to.

Stelle straightened her back, mindlessly flipping through the pages of a book, then snapped it shut.

"I wish I had my piano or my harp," she called loudly to the uninterested room, annoyed that no one was paying attention to her. She only had a few days left.

"You play the piano?" Ava asked from the door as she entered. She was wearing a soft green day dress; a little yellow flowered tiara sat on her head. Apparently, she'd noticed the dour mood as well and was doing her best to lighten things.

"You look nice today," Merrick said, holding Ava's hand and twirling her around. Jasper poured her a cup of tea, which she took, placing a kiss on Jasper's cheek. He frowned.

"I feel good today," Ava replied, then joined Stelle in the lounge, taking the chair across from her.

"Yes, I play many instruments, although I prefer strings. It's expected on Valtine." Stelle tilted her chin. She desperately missed the music of regular parties.

"I wish you'd told me sooner. Wait here a minute," Ava said, bouncing out of her chair and leaving Stelle to reminisce about balls and parties and everything she was missing.

Ava returned a short time later with a case, her hands shaking a little.

"You don't have to do this," Jasper said from the kitchen. "Stelle can entertain herself."

Her eyes were soft, and she placed her hand on his shoulder. "I want to. It'll be a pleasant distraction."

Ava came over to Stelle's chair and opened the case. Inside was a silver violin with green etchings along the edge. The strings squawked and squeaked as Ava adjusted the knobs.

When Ava started playing, the mood in the room lifted as the music flowed out smooth and clear like glass. It pulled at Stelle's heart, filled the room, and swam around them. Stelle was disappointed when it ended.

"Your turn," Ava said, handing the violin to Stelle. She doubted that there were many who could play as well as Ava. There was a natural ease to the sound she produced, but Stelle knew she wasn't without skill.

She ran the bow along the strings, purposefully extracting a low wail from them, and grinned wickedly at Merrick.

Then she played. The first song was fast, her fingers like lightning. For the next half hour, the only thing that mattered was the music: a low lullaby she had learned as a child, a haunting melody she'd play in the empty halls, an incredibly fast piece she'd committed to memory to impress her mother. She played until the tips of her fingers ached like they were going to bleed.

Stelle tried to get Ava to play again after each set, but each time Ava refused.

When her fingers could take no more, she stopped.

Merrick got up to rummage through the kitchen drawers. Then, sitting much too close, he passed Stelle a little jar of balm.

"Only two more days. How does it feel to be almost going in the right direction?" Merrick asked.

"Counting down the hours, I see." The room changed back to its usual grump once Stelle stopped playing. She rubbed the balm into the rough edges on the tips of her fingers, thankful he'd gotten it for her.

"No—not counting. I'm not sure the Lark will ever be the same again." His overly gallant words drew a chuckle from Stelle. If she was being honest with herself, she knew she would never be the same again either.

The room slowly emptied as everyone else went to bed, leaving Merrick and Stelle alone. She hid a yawn, not wanting to leave—not wanting the evening to be over.

The chaise felt smaller now that they were the only two people in the room. Stelle picked at the hem of her dress. The silence was heavy. She lifted her empty mug. Her fingers traced the black line around the top. She pretended to take a sip, then put it back down.

Merrick cleared his throat, and Stelle looked up, catching his eye. His features were soft and worn. And sad. Perhaps Ava was right about the sadness that he carried with him. She wanted to help, wanted to ask him so many questions—about his life, the pain he carried, how he ended up being captain of a salvage ship.

Her heart fluttered, wondering why she couldn't come up with a topic of conversation and why he wasn't saying anything either. He shifted towards her, leaving a hint of space between them. The hanging lights cast twinkling shadows around the room. She studied his unruly hair, the stubble on his jawline, and his dark eyes that remained focused on her.

His hand reached up, gently tracing along her cheek and tilting her chin. She leaned in.

Lavalle's voice heralded his approach. "If you think for one second Jasper's going to give you credit because you're the one that told him, then you haven't been listening to me all these years."

Stelle pulled back as if scalded. What had she almost done? Heat crept up the back of her neck; her cheeks flushed. Setting down the mug, she stood, retreating to where the violin and music sat out.

"I'm not trying to get credit." Sers's voice followed as both pilots entered.

Merrick stood and picked the cups up from the table.

"You know we have working comms," Merrick grumbled, placing the cups in the sink.

"Those crackled things?" Sers asked.

"Well, maybe we'll go back to the bridge and spend ten

minutes trying to reach you on a comm you don't even answer," Lavalle suggested.

"What did you want? Or was it Jasper you were looking for?"

Lavalle looked at Stelle and then whispered something to Merrick.

More muffled secrets that she was only a little curious about now.

Stelle put the violin back in its case, then placed the music sheets back in the box. Riffling through the sheets of music, she pretended to be sorting them. As she flitted through the music sheets, the top ones looked almost untouched. The ones underneath were worn and loved, with curled edges. All of them duets.

Stelle faked disinterest in their conversation. She caught bits about Tornillo and Jasper, but nothing discernible. She willed her heartbeat to stay steady as she tried to not wonder if Merrick had almost kissed her. It certainly seemed like he was going to kiss her. She did her best to focus on Merrick's intentions and not the very real feeling that she very much wanted him to.

Fifteen

Stelle watched from the bridge as they approached Tornillo. Like a giant corkscrew, the space station, ten times the size of a midway station, loomed before them. Ships of all sizes were docking or leaving, turning the corkscrew into a hive. She had a hard time believing that something so large didn't use Idex scans, and that Valtine courts allowed them to continue to function.

Sers and Lavalle buttoned up their shirts to the neck and donned long-fringed scarves. The soft scent of jasmine and spices followed them.

She'd made the mistake of commenting on their attire. As soon as she'd drawn attention to herself, they'd pressed her out of the bridge.

She made her way to the loading bay, carrying a small sack. Her red gown had never been properly washed and was now a permanent fixture under a pile of wires in Merrick's shop. She was happy to leave it behind. It was strange to carry so little with her.

Merrick was waiting at the first set of doors for Sers and

Lavalle to confirm that they'd docked.

Her fingers fluffed at a stray wisp of hair. Ava joined her, taking steps in a half skip.

"Lex's ship confirmed your passage, but you need to be there on time. They won't wait," Merrick said, going over the information he'd told her the night before. He pressed a small wallet into her hands, letting his hand linger for a second. Stelle ignored the little trill in her chest. "This will buy you some clothes and a few other things you might need, but stay away from the fancier stuff. You'll be back home soon enough, so it's safer right now to go for comfort. Ava will show you where to go. You won't be alone."

"I'm always alone," Stelle murmured. He slowly turned her rings, so the jewels faced into her palm.

"I suggest you don't wear those, or at least keep them hidden."

They'd been over the plan several times, including what she would say when she got home. No one on the Lark, including her, had any idea what would happen once her Idex hit the first scan in the hex-system. If there was one thing she was looking forward to, it was everyone's faces when she showed up for her first ball. Holding onto that happy thought, she squared her shoulders.

Goodbye. This was goodbye.

She hated it. Hated how much she cared. She had never cared about goodbyes. She'd left men swooning over her after parties, left her family to go on constant trips, left her maid, and left her friends. She never cared.

It was horrible to think, but she'd always felt others were losing someone with her departure. She had never felt like she might lose someone.

Merrick cleared his throat, took a step back, and let the door slide open.

"Come along, Ava," Stelle said, the hallway beckoning them forward. She walked toward the grey door at the end without looking back and immediately regretted it when the door closed behind her.

She walked down the connecting tunnel, sensing what little there was between her feet and infinite space. No different from a ship, she told herself, but walking across it made her legs weak.

The halls eventually opened into what she imagined was the centre of the corkscrew.

Stores lined the outer perimeter. Each store displayed a wide window and a tall doorway. Between the shops were grey doors, like the one she'd emerged from. Staggered stairs put each store on a different level. The long spiral of stores and grey doors slowly bent in a curve, up and down as far as she could see. Everything was too big and too small at the same time. Like a castle overstuffed with furniture, it tried to hold everything but left no room to navigate around the shoppers.

In the centre, a waterfall cascaded. She looked through the small bars of the railing and couldn't see its beginning or its end. Glowing orbs hovered in the waterfall. They sparkled and sent out little shoots of blue and purple light as the falling water pelted off of them.

Elaborate paintings covered door frames and trim in a bizarre display of planets, mountains, villages, and fruit, as if every inch of the place needed to be decorated. The sunny sky melted into a midnight motif. They passed closed shops with lowered lights or covered windows and other shops with wares piled so high they spilled into the hallway, narrowing the flow of traffic.

A hundred scents assaulted her at once—restaurants, cleaners, soaps, and the general smell of too many people in one place.

They passed a store with books piled to the ceiling and a ladder running between—Ava would probably want to stop there. But there was a list to be completed first.

Stelle paused for a moment in front of a barber shop. Men reclined in tilted chairs as they got a shave. The hint of ocean soaps made her think of her dad, and she wondered what he would say when she returned. Had he even mourned her?

"Did you need a shave?" Ava asked, coming up beside her. Stelle snickered. She was going to miss Ava.

Stelle remembered Merrick's instructions, and they passed by the fancier dress shops in search of something more useful. She wasn't supposed to stand out. Dozens of dresses hung on the wall in a mismatch of styles and colours. Some looked like hex-system fashion; others were completely foreign to her.

She wasn't sure why Merrick was so insistent about discreet clothing. There were men with fast trims, others in work uniforms. She saw ladies with hats so tall it prevented them from walking safely between aisles and others wearing black pants and laced boots.

They entered a shop with low lighting, likely to mask the inferior stitch quality. Instead of mannequins with glamorous outfits and a modiste to fit her, there were items folded and small displays showing what was in each stack.

Stelle chose a few items and squeezed into the fitting room.

Black pants with tight pockets hugged her curves and fit nicely into a pair of the navy laced boots. She added a few light-blue tops and undergarments. They were plain, but it was going to be lovely to have something that fit well. Then she chose a slightly nicer travelling outfit. The skirt was long and burgundy, with glitter; a black top matched. She came out wearing the clothing she'd bought and an armload of others.

The coins Merrick gave her were heavy as she passed them to the owner. She rarely held actual currency, as she always billed purchases to one of her estates.

At the next stop, she decided there was enough money to get some new soaps and lotions.

Stelle stood in front of a red-lit shelf with a row of cosmetics. The woman at the counter wore no makeup but sported a tall hat with large feathers. Around the far side of the cosmetics counter, a row of equally ostentatious hats towered. The woman barely acknowledged their entrance and kept picking at the crack on the counter.

Clearly, no one was going to help. There were palettes of various colours and glitters as well as some more subtle tones, which she always gravitated towards.

"This blush would bring some colour to your cheeks," Stelle said. "You're so pale all the time." Trial brush in hand, she took Ava's chin and applied the blush. Once she realized they could try whatever they wanted without supervision, she had Ava done up in minutes, then went to fixing her hair high.

"Oh, I'm fancy," Ava said, admiring herself in the mirror.

"Exactly like a lady, I think," Stelle said as she applied some sparkle to her own lids.

"A lady? Idex doesn't matter out here," Ava reminded her.

"It doesn't, which means no one will know or care. I couldn't imagine being friends with someone who's not a lady, and therefore you're a lady," Stelle stated and plopped the fancy yellow netted hat on Ava's head.

Stelle put the coins on the counter, hoping it was the correct amount. The woman nodded and waved them off.

Ava strode out of the cosmetics store, a stern frown on her face. "I, Lady Ava, demand everyone stop and pay attention to me!" she commanded and then giggled, her face lit with the fun of it. Her voice barely carried, but it was enough to get a few eye rolls and the scrutiny of two men who stood off to the side watching them.

"Perhaps we're drawing too much attention," Stelle said, taking Ava's arm and hurrying her along.

They strode up the ever-ascending hall of stores for a few more minutes and then back down again. Stelle purchased everything she needed, and it was time to part.

"I guess this is where we say goodbye," Ava said, bringing her up near the end of the shops.

"One more…" Stelle grabbed Ava's hand and dragged her into the bookstore she'd spied when they first arrived. Ava nodded, obviously happy to be around so many books. Stelle didn't know what to look for. There was a portly man seated at the counter. Much like the cosmetics store, he didn't even glance up when they entered.

Ava walked aimlessly, running her hands along the spines. She wasn't even looking at them.

Stelle found one with a nice cover, which was enough to make her want to buy it herself.

Sneaking to the counter, she paid for it quickly with her last coin, then tucked it under her arm. As they exited, she held it out for Ava.

"I'm not sure I'll even have time to finish the one I'm on," Ava said, but held onto it and stroked the cover.

"You have nothing but time, stuck on your ship for who knows how long," Stelle said, insisting.

Ava hugged her fiercely, then let go. Goodbye took too long and was over too fast. Stelle hated the ache in her chest as Ava walked away.

Within the hour, the Lark would be gone, and she was to be at a door marked 893. They would ask her a question, and she'd have a password. It was silly. No one had looked at her twice since they'd arrived.

A few short hours and she'd be heading home.

Stelle made her way through the shops she'd already seen, then back again. This section was lit like sunshine. Its bright walls and white crystals glittered. These shops were slightly higher end. She passed a music shop. A row of violins hung along the back wall.

Her meagre funds were all gone, but she wanted to admire the violins.

The store owner was a tall, willowy-looking woman in a pink spun dress.

"That one," Stelle said, pointing to the far left. It was made of a red-brown wood with violets inlaid around the top. The shopkeeper reluctantly held it out to her.

The moment she touched the instrument, she knew Ava needed to have it. The book wasn't a big enough gift at all. She could double back and find her quickly. Slowly turning one of her rings, she pulled it off her finger.

"Will this cover the cost?" Stelle asked, knowing she was breaking one of Merrick's rules about showing her jewels.

The woman eyed her, then snatched the ring from her hand. Pulling out a small tool, she ran it over the ring. Her eyes widened, and Stelle knew she'd gotten the lower end of the bargain. She didn't care. She'd replace it when she got home.

The woman hurriedly packaged up the violin as if Stelle were going to change her mind. The passage to the Lark wasn't far, and Ava might not even be back yet.

Running back through the halls, she got some odd looks. She wasn't sure if she should go all the way to the Lark. She could simply say she was delivering another package. Merrick didn't even need to know she'd broken the rules she'd promised to follow.

Passing the bookstore, she stopped short. Ava was at the counter. Stelle watched for a moment and then saw her return the book she'd bought her. The clerk furrowed his brow but nodded and handed the coin back to Ava. Stelle knew little about books. It probably wasn't to Ava's taste. Stelle's face flushed, and anger burned where she held the violin against her heart.

Stelle paced back and forth between the two stores, occasionally bumping into people when she pivoted too fast. She wanted to confront Ava but knew it didn't matter; they wouldn't even know each other after this. She hated how it bothered her so much. Pausing, she leaned against the wall. Perhaps it was simply one of those times where she'd completely missed what was going on. Maybe the violin would be a terrible gift too. She wasn't even sure she wanted to give it to her anymore.

Hesitating, she saw two men approach Ava as she left the store. They were fairly tall, well-built and in plain clothes, but clean looking. Ava walked away from them, but within a second there was a third man wearing a long black coat. He held Ava's arm, whispered something in her ear, then pushed her forward.

Ava paled. Her eyes searched furiously as they guided her through the sea of people

Stelle held her breath, not sure what to do. The air felt heavy, squeezing out of her lungs the way it had when they'd passed the solar flares. Forcing her lungs to expand and take in oxygen, she followed them down the hallway. Descending the spiral, they passed the shops, restaurants, and entered an area with boarded-up stores. The crowd thinned.

She kept back, not losing sight of them but not daring to get any closer, debating what she should do. If she went back to the Lark, she wouldn't know where they'd taken Ava. If she cried out now, they could hurt Ava or even turn and attack her.

A curse escaped her lips.

There was no way she could follow them onto a ship. Her heart lurched as they left the hallway for one of the grey doors. They were leaving the centre of the corkscrew. Stelle followed.

She lost them for a minute, heart pounding. No longer in the central spiral, she had no idea where she was.

The man she mentally dubbed Long-coat turned and entered what looked like an old pub. Thankfully, it didn't appear to be connected to a ship.

Breath filled her lungs as she drew in the heavy air. They

hadn't noticed her. She should turn back and tell Merrick, but what if they didn't stay in the abandoned shop?

Stelle squared her shoulders. What had space done to her? She was Lady Cristelle, not some frail shipmate. If she wanted Ava back safe and sound, then it was Ava she was going to get.

Pushing all rational doubt from her mind, she pressed the unlock button and opened the door.

Sixteen

In a busy bar at the bottom of Tornillo, Merrick rested his dark brew on the silver half-moon table and tugged the sleeve of his uniform. Barons, this well-to-do establishment, gave off a welcoming glow with its low lights and wall sconces. The silver tables and crystal chandelier reflected off the glass floor. Its genuine appeal was that being at the bottom of Tornillo meant Barons boasted a unique view of the waterfall above. The water sloshed and swirled as it was pumped back to the top. Between the waves, glimpses of space contrasted with the swirl of lights within the water.

Most people kept to themselves, which suited him fine. He didn't want anyone too interested in what was going on at his table. Sers and Lavalle sauntered into Barons right on time to provide Merrick with an extra layer of distraction.

They approached the busy bar that stretched across the far edge and ordered their golden haze. Within minutes, Merrick could hear them telling stories, some of which might have been true. Most were, at the very least, exaggerated. The bartender pretended to clean a crystal bowl and leaned toward them.

Light laughter rose, and Sers leaned back in his chair with a smug look on his face that was quickly turned down at whatever Lavalle said next.

Merrick relaxed in his seat, waiting for his contact to arrive. He tried to push worry for Stelle out of his mind.

Taking a sip, Merrick scanned the room and resisted the urge to check his timepiece.

A portly man sat down across from him. Blonde hair swept to one side and brushed over his eye, doing little to hide a scar that ran across his brow.

"Can I help you?" Merrick asked. This man was nervous, and too conspicuous.

"You're not Captain Merrick?" The man's eyes bulged in fear. He fumbled as he tried to stand.

"I am. Sit down. And calm down before you draw attention. Look around. No one here cares about us or what we're talking about," Merrick said.

The man let out a breath. Placing his elbows on the table, he leaned forward. "You going to drink that?" he asked.

Merrick slid the brew toward him and waited as he took a long drink, sloshing brown drops over the edge of his mouth. Wiping his face with the back of his sleeve, he let out a heavy sigh. Being seen with anyone from the crew of the Sevona—another salvage ship—was a risk. This meeting was to exchange information, but clearly something had gone wrong.

"I'm part of the cleaning crew. I was off the Sevona when it happened. The entire crew was compromised." His hands shook. Pulling a small round data-disc out of his side pocket, he slid it across the table.

Merrick picked up the empty glass and data-disc in one

smooth move, stood, and then brought the glass to the bar, hoping the man had the common sense to stay where he was. Dropping the disc into Lavalle's side pocket, he ordered another round and returned to his seat.

"Tell me what happened," Merrick said. He stretched his legs and, this time, took a long drink.

"I always knew about the plan, but I'm still just part of the cleaning crew. An ambassador boarded with a whole swag of men. They were looking for someone named Lady Daye. Well, we didn't know anything about it, but they scanned each member. I guess it's a big secret that this Daye is missing, because they didn't run a full scan on Tornillo—but they looked official enough to. Now they know exactly who everyone on the Sevona is, except for me. We unloaded scrap and pretended all was normal, but they didn't want to meet up with you—not after their Idexes were logged as being on Tornillo."

The chance of the Lark's crew being scanned at the same time as the Sevona's was unlikely, but Merrick was thankful for the caution.

"Can you relay a message?"

The man nodded, the blonde hairs bouncing in unison.

"Tell them to stay neutral: pick up space junk, make a little coin. Don't answer any calls. We'll set up a meet on Corva. I'll transmit it through the regular channels once enough time has passed."

The man's shoulders relaxed, and he nodded. Relief flooded across his eyes, and he almost smiled. Taking a ship out of commission for a time wasn't ideal, but if the information they needed was on the data-disc, then it was worth it.

Seventeen

Stelle raised her eyebrow in perfect indifference. In the same way she would glide into a ballroom, she strode into the abandoned pub. The smell of mouldy fruits and stale haze coiled around her.

A quick survey of the room didn't help Stelle form a plan. The shortest of the three men was heading toward the bar and had his back turned when she entered the room. He turned towards her, mouth hanging open in surprise. A faded black shirt pulled tightly across his midsection. He was unlikely to be the biggest obstacle—he had a lazy look about him.

Long-coat stood beside Ava. The coat would have been intimidating, but his arms didn't fill out the sleeves. The third man wore a blue-and-green duster with rows of fringe, and stood on the other side of Ava. He had sharp, chiselled features that could have almost been handsome if Stelle wasn't so angry. Ava looked frail and breakable between the hardy men.

Instead of addressing the men, she brushed past them as if she didn't see them, bumping into Long-coat and making him stumble to the side.

Statues, she told herself. They were statues, so far below her.

"How dare you leave me with this to carry? I didn't hire you to loaf about!" Stelle shoved the bags at Ava, transferring the weight of the packages to Ava's hands. It forced Ava's arm free from Fringe's loose grip.

"Take them!" Stelle screeched as one bag threatened to drop. She manoeuvred herself as a shield around Ava. With her shoulders now in the space Ava had previously occupied, she propelled the girl toward the door.

Ava let out a strangled sound, wrapping her fingers over the package handles. Stelle knew she didn't have long. Quick action would replace the confusion she'd caused.

Long-coat righted himself and in two steps moved to block their departure.

"Gentlemen," she said, her voice low and sharp, "if you'll excuse us, this girl owes me a debt. I'll return her to you when it's paid."

"Well now, looks like we almost made a blunder. You carry yourself like a lady," he said, then spit on the carpet. It left an uneven stain as it soaked in.

"We were told to take the lady. He pointed them out and said to take the lady," the one Stelle had named Lazy stammered. He had yet to move closer to help his companions, but his eyes darted nervously between them.

Ava's yellow hat tilted to one side and the feathers draped over her eye. A pang of regret shoot through her. Someone had hired these men to take a lady, and Stelle had indulged the stupid notion of dressing Ava up as one.

"Lovely timing. Looks like we have two for the trouble of one." Long-coat shrugged.

"Oh darling, I don't think you know who I am," Stelle said. She stepped closer, looked him in the eye, and pressed a finger into his chest. "I'm trouble for twenty."

Then Stelle executed a move Lady Lucy had helped her perfect in the ballroom. One foot slid to the side and the other one slid forward as if she'd nearly fainted. With both arms up, she fell forward into Long-coat.

Acting on instinct, he caught her and tried to restrain the flailing arms. Unsure of what to do, he let her weight pull on his arms.

Stelle looked at Ava, who was stunned and not moving, and mouthed the word *run*.

Confusion was how Stelle had rescued her sister off the dance floor on many occasions. The routine was familiar, like a second skin. The indifference, the confidence, the fake faint, and the swift movements had worked.

Lifting her foot, she kicked high, her toe reaching the release on the door. Stelle spun away from the flowing dark folds of Long-coat and pushed Ava out. Once Ava was in the hallway, Stelle made a fist and slammed the door lock.

With her back pressed flat against the door, Stelle splayed her hands over the cold metal and gathered her thoughts. This dance was about to take a dark turn. Ava was in the hallway and the confusion had cleared. She needed to buy Ava some time to get away.

Long-coat charged at her, but she brought her elbow up, connecting with his jaw, and then kneed him as hard as she could.

Eighteen

Merrick waited for a peal of laughter from Sers and Lavalle before getting up and slipping out of Barons.

Hands in his pockets, he drew no attention as he pressed through the crowded hallway on his way back to the Lark.

He tried not to search the crowds for Stelle. He wanted to make sure she was okay, but checking on her was impossible. Merrick had prepared her for any possibility. Stelle had been unconcerned and confident. She was going home, and no one was going to prevent that from happening.

When he reached the Lark, Ruse was pacing in the loading bay.

"Ava's not returned," Ruse said. Merrick checked his timepiece. She was a few minutes late, but so were Jasper and his pilots. There wasn't a cause for alarm yet. Merrick inspected Ruse. His hair was unruly, like he had run his hand through it a dozen times. He strained to look past Merrick to see if anyone else was coming.

Before Merrick could comment on Ruse's unusual concern, Ava stumbled through the enclosed walkway and into the loading bay. Tears were streaming down her cheeks and a cry of relief slipped past her lips when she saw them. A dozen packages weighed her down. She faltered as Merrick sprinted toward her. He reached out, supporting her as much as possible with the bags still in the way. Merrick shook her hands gently, until the packages came loose from her grasp and fell to the metal floor.

"Stelle needs us, and she told me I had to take the packages. We can't leave them on the floor," Ava cried. Grabbing the edges of Merrick's shirt, she balled the loose fabric in her hands and sobbed.

Merrick held onto her for a moment, speaking calmly and waiting for the sobs to turn into a steady cry.

"What did Stelle do? I told you taking gifts from her would come to no good!" Ruse spat, fury rolling off him. His eyes darted wildly between the packages and Ava.

Ava pushed away from Merrick at the sound of Ruse's voice. Kneeling on the floor, she tried to gather the bags.

"You told me to return the book, that a gift from a lady was a betrayal of what we do—that I was silly for thinking of her as my friend… but she saved me."

Ruse pushed her aside and lifted the bags in one easy swoop, stopping Ava's efforts. Merrick reached out for Ava again and let the bulk of her weight lean against him.

None of this was making sense. He waited a minute for Ava's sobs to calm, then had her start at the beginning. Ava spoke in a long stream of words, including the explanation for the yellow feather disaster on her head. His heart thundered when Ava explained how they'd taken her, understanding her panic.

"We need to get moving," Ruse stated. "If someone has Stelle, they could easily track her to the Lark."

"What happened?" Jasper's voice boomed from the cargo hold.

"Stelle got mistaken for Lady Daye, and it's none of our concern," Ruse said.

Merrick tried to block out the noise around him so he could focus, pulling apart the problem in front of him.

"They might know where the Lark is already," Ruse said, his voice a low growl.

"That's not possible. We've taken every precaution," Jasper said, his double blade flickering like lightning between his fingers. "But we do have to leave now. We can't have both ships docked at the same time."

Merrick watched Jasper's knife, his own thoughts like sharp edges piercing through one possibility after another. The noise dimmed, and all eyes turned to Merrick, who was looking directly at Ruse.

"I thought you stayed with the Lark," Merrick asked. A tiny loose thread poked out from all the possible scenarios, and Merrick pulled it.

"I did," Ruse said. He was staring past Merrick, not making eye contact.

"No, you ran into me and told me to return the book," Ava said, then put her hand over her mouth and looked at Ruse.

"I'm allowed to leave the ship," Ruse said, defending himself. He shifted the packages still in his grip and looked forward to the inside of the Lark, then back to the opening to Tornillo. "Why do you care so much? People like her are the reason we're out here. You all act like heroes, saving her from the Monrovia explosion, then saving her from poison. She deserves every bad thing that happens to her."

Merrick's heart sank, thinking back to the incident with the poisoned tea. Ruse had never come to the dining room when Ava had called for help. Merrick also knew that he hadn't yet told anyone about the search for Lady Daye on Tornillo. Staring at Ruse, he didn't want to believe it. They'd been sailing together for over a year now. He knew Ruse was passionate about what they were doing, especially after Helen died, but it made little sense to blame Stelle directly.

"Did you contact them before or after you found out someone was searching for Lady Daye?" Jasper asked, clearly on the same page as Merrick.

"The fates lined it up. They handed me the chance. I just did what you all wanted to do, but couldn't bring yourselves to. She's wearing Helen's dresses, and she's a *lady*. Don't act like I did something wrong. I know how much Jasper hates her, and how she annoys Merrick—"

Sers and Lavalle broke into the hull. Lavalle cut his laugh short when he saw Ava's tears and the deadly look on Jasper's face. Ruse kicked the packages at Lavalle, pushing past them and back down the tunnel to Tornillo.

"Sers, I need you to get Ava back to her room. Lavalle, get my ship moving," Merrick said. Needing no further explanation, Lavalle ran toward the bridge.

Merrick looked to where Ruse had fled. Recalling every interaction Ruse had had with Stelle, he should have seen that the indifference was masking something deeper.

A dozen problems sprang to mind. He would need to reset so many protocols and hope Ruse wouldn't betray them further.

He also needed to decide quickly what to do about Stelle. Merrick knew there were a dozen reasons they should just leave. She was a lady, which meant ransom was a possibility. They had already saved her and done more than they should. If Jasper was thinking the same thing, this was going to be more difficult.

"You have a plan?" Jasper asked.

"I do, but you might not like it."

The door closed, sealing them off from Tornillo.

Disengaging from the dock, the Lark quietly slipped back into space.

Nineteen

Stelle watched as the three men shouted at each other. One went for the door, while the other lunged for her. Outmatched in every way, with no chance for escape, Stelle prepared for a fight.

The man she decided to call Fringe took a slap to the face before pinning Stelle's arms to her side. The scent of stale socks rubbed off on her new clothing. She dug her nails into his hand, which made him release her. Long-coat was close beside and took over where Fringe had failed. His knee came up and jabbed her in the ribs, doubling her over, and before she'd recovered, a knife was pressed against her throat.

"He paid us to get rid of you," Long-coat said in a growl.

"I'll check the hall," Fringe said, rubbing his jaw. Opening the door, he looked out, turning his head in both directions before coming back in.

"She's gone. Did you want me to follow?"

"No—by now she'll be on the main floor. We need to move."

"We can't kill her now," said Lazy from the bar area, eyes

wide. "They're going to come looking for her."

"We were never going to kill her," Fringe said.

"But we got paid to," Lazy said. He came out from behind the counter with a blue bottle. Dusting it off, he filled a cup with liquid. The dark grey sludge looked like it had separated into a dozen parts, then remixed.

Stelle smelled the mustiness of the ancient haze as he brought it close. She bucked against the man holding her, but the knife pressed into her neck, cutting into her skin. The smallest drop of blood dripped down her neck and onto her new black shirt.

Fringe opened a little container from inside his jacket. He sprinkled the powdery contents on top of the haze, then stirred it with his finger. Wiping the excess onto his pants, he stepped toward her.

Stelle tried to not retch as Fringe lifted the glass to her lips and poured the haze into her mouth. The knife twitched, daring her to move.

"Be a good girl," Long-coat said. "You drink up, and we won't have to kill you."

The haze burned in the back of her throat.

"I thought you said we weren't going to kill her?" Lazy asked, earning a glare from his companions. Stelle looked between the three as the room swayed. She rarely drank haze, but a little mouthful never bothered her. Reaching out for the container in Fringe's pocket, her weight pulled, causing her side to ache. She could steal it and see what it was, if she could get close enough.

"How much did you give her?" Long-coat asked. Her weight sagged against him, and she no longer cared about the smell floating around her. The coloured bottles glowed and tilted. She wondered if she could steal the little bottles, the way she'd stolen Lord Featherson's cuff links on the Monrovia. Thoughts of petty thievery danced around as she tried to bring her mind back to the present. She grabbed at the black edges of Long-coat's coat, steadying herself.

"The way she was fighting, I figured we didn't want to take any chances," he replied.

"I'm a lady," she mumbled. "I'm worth more than your space station."

Stelle wasn't sure who was speaking now as they half dragged her through a back door. She hoped Ava had found a lift to carry the bags back to the Lark. They were too heavy for her.

The memory of Ava bolted through her scattered thoughts. Safe. Ava was safe. Stelle smiled and leaned against the wall, wishing she could curl up on the floor. She reached down for the silver tiles with sparkling blue flecks. Long-coat held her at her waist as she brushed her fingertips across the floor. He yanked on her stomach, and she straightened.

The lift continued its climb. Stelle remembered seeing Tornillo from the outside—it could dock a thousand ships. But Merrick had prepared her, hadn't he? What was she supposed to do if something went wrong? She couldn't remember what she was supposed to do.

Stelle's hand was swelling. She stretched out each finger, still able to move them all. Her side ached, probably from a fractured rib. She lifted her shirt to check but then pulled it back down. Now was not the time.

When the lift finally stopped, they brought her to a parlour.

The carpet was an ocean of mauve cluttered with rose tufted chairs. They lowered her down onto a pink cushion.

"I don't like her being here. This wasn't part of the plan," Fringe said.

She looked up from under her dark lashes. He sounded nervous. She liked nervousness; it was something she could work with. Stelle tried to focus on the men, but the mauve carpet swam up and swallowed them all before spitting them back out.

"I sent out an open-bid. She'll be off our hands—"

Stelle looked at Long-coat's hands, but they'd sprouted puffy pink pillows.

They talked and moved and came in and out of the room, all in what felt like seconds. Like lightning, moments flashed and then were gone, leaving a dull roar of thunder confusing her.

"Wake up," Lazy said and kicked Stelle's feet.

However much time had passed, it was not enough to clear Stelle's thoughts. Holding back tears, she refused to feel sorry for herself. She had to get home.

"We've got a fancy buyer lined up, so look presentable," Lazy said and gave her another kick, which Stelle returned.

Everything slid sideways, and then she was back in her room on Valtine. Stelle looked at the row of dresses that hung in front of a mirrored wall. They stretched beyond the white pillars and sank into her polished sapphire floors.

Stelle tried to yell at her maid to help her find the wall. She hated the sound. Why did she do it? Her skin was burning and cold at the same time. Like it wasn't her own.

The words filtered in, but they sounded like men, not like

her maids.

"This is what you're offering?" The man's voice was low.

She knew his voice, but he shouldn't be in her room. It wasn't her father's voice. Who was he? The weight of her head kept her from looking up as she stared at his shoes. They were black and shiny. Like ballroom shoes. Like a lord would wear. She inspected the stitching around the edges. It was masterfully done and carried a soft V crest woven with vines around the toe.

Stelle knew that crest. Those were Valtine shoes.

No, she wasn't on Valtine, she tried to remind herself.

She was on Tornillo. But those shoes were definitely here with her. She tried to reach down to touch one, but he pulled his toe back from her. Whoever the buyer was, he had money and good taste.

"I'm not taking her if she can't walk," the man sniffed. She could walk. She tried to straighten herself up. She wanted to go with the nice shoes.

"I can walk," Stelle said. Her voice was scratchy and far away. Her legs weak, she forced herself to stand, but a rough hand pushed her back down into the chair.

Payment passed in front of her. She was forced to stand, just as she'd been trying to only moments before.

Then she was leaving the mauve room and following the man with the glorious shoes. She wanted to touch them and tried kneeling down to run her hands over the shine of the black.

"I need you to stand as tall as you can and walk," the voice said. She knew the voice. Standing, she leaned against him. She didn't want to lean against him. He was straight and strong. His voice—so familiar, but he was wearing the wrong shoes.

"I know you can't, but you have to. Do you hear me? Lady Cristelle…"

Her name … she hadn't heard it in so long.

"Lady Cristelle—I need you to walk!"

"Lord Terrington? Jasper?" Stelle tried to control the flood of memories that flew through her mind like dragonflies, zigzagging their way around. She squared her shoulders. The way he said her name … why he'd avoided her on the Lark… she'd been a young woman when she'd met him, but she remembered now.

The doors opened, and in front of her there were other people. This was why she couldn't stagger. She needed to appear normal.

Because Jasper needed her to be.

She knew him. He must have picked up on the flash of recognition. "Not yet—you need to stay calm and focused."

Stelle nodded.

"Ava?" Stelle asked quietly.

"Safe—keep walking."

Grey door number 962. At the end of the hallway was a port with a docked ship. Jasper led her into the back; it was no bigger than her safety pod. All black interior with aqua lights and soft seats, it was big enough for only the two of them and open to the pilot seat where Sers sat. She wanted to throw her arms around the pilot and kiss his cheek, but she barely made it to a seat before the door sealed.

Stelle shook as they detached from the satellite, and once again she rocketed into space.

Except this time she wasn't alone.

"I like your shoes," she said to Jasper, then dropped to her knees and threw up all over them.

Twenty

Stelle woke with a splitting headache. Her neck and side hurt. A lump on the back of her head throbbed. Someone pressed a cold cloth over her eyes. The compress was heavily doused in herbs and peppermint, but it was too medicinal to be pleasant.

She waved off whoever was with her and received a low chuckle in return.

"Stop trying to dismiss me. I need to change the compress on your side," Merrick said. His voice rumbled through the room. Stelle was certain she'd never heard a nicer voice in her life.

"Ava?" Stelle asked as she tried to sit up. A wave of nausea hit her, and Merrick gently lowered her back down. His rough fingers trailed the edge of her bruised ribs, and he repositioned the cold pack.

"I think we might need the doctor to take another look at this. Ava's safe. It might not feel like it, but you're safe too."

Stelle wrinkled her nose at the heavy mint smell, but the potent combination worked fast, easing the pain.

"You came back for me?" Stelle asked.

"Yes, we came back for you."

Stelle tried to hold back another wave of nausea as the medicinal effects overtook her and she drifted back to sleep.

When she woke again, she was alone. Light poured from an open door, illuminating the bedroom. Like the other rooms on the Lark, it was open and inviting. Dark cherry wood lined the walls. Cupboards with golden, gear-shaped knobs separated the sleeping area from a sitting room. The bed was large. A cot stretched out beside it, with its own set of cushions and blankets. She frowned at the cot, hoping she didn't snore in her sleep.

She tossed off the plush navy blanket, steadied herself, and went to the adjoining bathroom.

In the centre of the captain's bathroom, beside a pile of fluffy towels, was a shower. This whole time, Merrick had had a private shower. Somehow she liked him more because he'd kept it from her; or perhaps her lack of annoyance was the relief of being back on the Lark. Her ribs ached as she changed out of her clothing and stepped under the waterfall.

Stelle lathered herself in his soaps, washing off the day's events. The orange-and-spice scent reminded her of warm summer breezes and fruit plates on the top of Valtine castles. And yet there was no place she'd rather be than on the Lark.

Wrapping a towel around herself, she noticed the bin outside the bathroom door. It held the new clothing she had purchased on Tornillo, packages that Ava should have dropped.

The soft purple lounge pants flowed around her legs like silk, and the fitted top made her feel almost normal. She brushed her hair long and towel dried it, then curled back up in the bed.

Water seeped from her hair onto the pillow, leaving a large wet blot. She turned it over, soaking the dry side a little slower, then switched it for the one on the cot beside her and drifted back to sleep.

When she woke for the third time, the room was still dark. Merrick was sleeping on the cot beside the bed. His eyes opened as she shifted. Without his overcoat, Stelle could see a long scar running from his shoulder all the way down his left arm. She wanted to trace the line and ask about it. His gaze caught hers and held it for a moment.

"Are you okay?" Merrick asked.

No, she wasn't okay. Everything hurt. Her stomach was churning, and someone had tried to kill her—again—and home was now even farther out of reach.

"I'm fine," Stelle murmured.

His hand reached over the gap between the two beds and rested on her shoulder. She wanted to pull his arm over her cold and aching body. She wanted to pull his cot closer until she could feel the warmth from his body shielding her. Instead, she lay still, pretending she'd fallen back asleep.

The next morning, Stelle left Merrick's rooms and made her way to the kitchen. The room was quiet, but there was a little note beside a cup of tea and a plate of food waiting for her on the table.

She winced as she lowered herself into the seat, swirled the lukewarm tea around the bottom of her mug, and thought about Merrick. The long scar, the personal shower, the flutter in her stomach when he rested his hand protectively on her shoulder. She replayed it and let herself imagine what it would be like to curl up against him. She also thought how utterly inappropriate all of those thoughts were for a lady. But thoughts of Merrick were better than memories of Tornillo. Between sleeping Merrick filled her in on what had happened, and that Ruse was gone. Every time her thoughts drifted back to the space station, her chest tightened, but Merrick was there.

Beside a half-full plate of fresh fruit and cheese lay a discarded book. Stelle sat down at the table and picked it up. Fanning the pages, she let them dust over her fingers like flower petals.

Jasper entered the kitchen and nodded his head in her direction before kneeling down to rummage through the lower cupboards. He was wearing his well-fitted coveralls, gloves sticking out of the back pocket. He appeared ordinary—not at all like the Valtine lord she remembered. Although, as she watched him now, she noticed the coveralls were a little too fitted, and the fabric was somewhat fine for the type of work he did.

"What are you looking for?" Stelle asked, taking a bite of the sliced cheese. She wished she had a fresh cup of tea to go with it, but the thought of her aching ribs and distance from her chair to the kitchen gave her pause.

"I was looking for polish for my shoes." He straightened and held up a small coal-coloured jar, then tucked it into his pocket and turned on the kettle.

Stelle held the book at eye level to hide her embarrassment

at the remembrance of throwing up on those shoes and flipped the pages, pretending to read. They must have taken some time to clean.

"What Ruse did to you was wrong, and you did a good thing," Jasper said, handing her a hot cup of tea.

"Don't be ridiculous. If I hadn't made Ava pretend to be a lady, they would have taken me away, and you never would have known."

She shook as the words came out, the familiar tightness in her chest coming back. If they hadn't taken Ava by mistake, no one would have known to rescue her.

The cup rattled against the wood as she tried to set it down. Jasper put his hands over hers to stop the trembling. Stelle pulled back and stared at Jasper's mug. It was the plain grey one from the back of the cupboard. Lord Terrington never would have been seen using such a simple mug.

Jasper—Lord Terrington—had left Valtine when she was young. He was renowned for his extravagant parties. She'd never been old enough to receive an invitation. The introduction had happened when she was staying on one of Lady Daye's estates for a summer. Stelle knew Lady Daye had been in love with Jasper, but he'd left without a trace, and now he was sitting across from her.

"What happened to you?" Stelle asked.

"Valtine didn't suit me," Jasper said. He took a long drink of tea, placed the drab mug on the table, and leaned back.

"Does Merrick know who you are?"

"Yes, Merrick knows I'm a Valtine lord."

"Is that why he doesn't use titles on the ship? Because you outrank him?" Stelle asked.

"I don't outrank Merrick," Jasper said, a little stiffly.

Stelle's mouth hung open for a minute, then she shut it and pressed her lips together. She'd missed the signs of Jasper being from Valtine, but there was no way Merrick was.

"Who is he?" Stelle asked.

"He's a mechanic from Koros—one of the poorest planets in the outer systems. And I don't outrank him. No one does. Not you. Not anyone in your Valtine court—" Jasper sounded like he was going to start a lecture when Sers entered. He was wearing his usual beige pants and red top; his fluffy white, untrimmed sideburns stuck out in a scraggly mess.

"Don't let him fool you. He was all high and mighty when Merrick saved him. Jasper thought he could pilot a dart—couldn't even get it off the ground. Merrick was just a young snapper, but he pulled Jasper out of a burning scrap pile."

"I remember the flounder dart," Lavalle said, coming in not far behind. He pulled a chair away from the table and joined them. Reaching over, he patted Stelle's hand. "Jasper woke up in the sick bay claiming to be some sort of king, lovesick over losing someone named Lady Daye."

Stelle dropped her gaze, pretending not to hear Lady Daye's name, and stole a glance at Jasper. A pained look crossed his eyes for a moment before he recovered himself.

"That's not half as bad as the state he found you two in," Jasper countered.

The bickering broke out and then settled into a broken form of storytelling. The mood on the Lark shifted, and stories filled the next hour.

From bits of each story, Stelle pieced together the history of the Lark's crew. Jasper had left for the outer planets on commission from the Valtine court. Stelle questioned how this could be possible because Valtine lords did not take commissions, but she was sure Jasper had lowered himself to get away from Lady Daye. Sers and Lavalle had both been pilots during a conflict on Koros. It was unclear who'd been on what side, or what the conflict was even about, but Stelle got the distinct feeling it didn't matter. Merrick had, in one way or another, rescued them all and brought them together.

Stelle's side ached as the cold compress lost its effect. She needed a new one but didn't want to ask any of the men who were regaling her with their stories of heroism. Perhaps it was time she went to see the mysteriously absent doctor for herself.

Twenty-One

After sitting for so long, the pain in her ribs had become almost overwhelming. She leaned against the wall for a minute, taking in shallow breaths and waiting for the aches to subside before continuing her search for the doctor.

Stelle was at least enjoying the advantages of the Lark not having Idex trackers at every entrance. Previously, if she wanted to get into a restricted area, she needed a group of people and a reason to do it.

Besides, she was still Lady Cristelle, and if she wanted to see the ship's doctor, then that was what she would do.

She had long suspected that the Lark was a twin ship with mirrored sides. It was the only way to explain the smaller dart that had picked her up on Tornillo—and the fact that there was a doctor whom she still hadn't met. For all she knew, there could be a whole other crew living on the opposite side.

Stelle pocketed Jasper's security card when he refilled her tea, promising herself she would give it back when she was done. Then, claiming to be tired, she left them to their stories. A small shiver of excitement slinked down her spine as she tried the first door. To her dismay it was nothing more than a large storage room full of neatly stacked bins. Stelle let out a sigh, opening the second door, expecting to find more storage. Instead she was thrilled as a short access point between the two sides of the ship opened before her. After taking a quick look behind her, she slipped through the opening and closed the door.

Gone were the soft carpets and panelled walls. Grey floors, bright lights, and sterile white walls replaced the comfort of the living quarters. Her stocking feet padded softly as she wandered the halls, eventually coming to an opening similar in size to their lounge area. Instead of fancy furnishings, there were a dozen units filled with empty beds lined with crisp white sheets. Glass shelves lined the walls. The room smelled clean and too much like the compresses she'd been using.

Stelle walked the length to the end. Strapped to the wall was a long silver pod with a frosted glass top. She drew her arms across her chest as she approached, reading Helen's name on the readout panel. Ava's friend, Ruse's sweetheart. Stelle wasn't sure why she'd assumed the body wouldn't be on the Lark—but there it was. A chill spread up her arms and tingled the back of her neck.

The feeling she was being watched fell heavy over her, and she peered into the frosted glass.

"Don't touch that!" a voice boomed through the medical bay.

Stelle shot up straight and turned.

The man's black shirt stretched over well-muscled arms. Peppered-grey hair and a scowl gave him a distinguished look.

"Dr Moss?" Stelle exclaimed, brow furrowed. Shock

jumbled her thoughts as she tried to place this man on the Lark. "But you're in prison."

"Obviously."

"No—but you are. You're on Orion." Stelle struggled to accept that the man in front of her was Dr Moss. He had lived on the Obsidian for years. He'd been taken into custody after leaving the Obsidian to aid Wynter.

"As far as anyone is concerned, I'm still there."

Stelle straightened the sleeves on her floral top. She was wearing one of the simple day outfits from Tornillo and wished now that she'd worn something fancier—at the very least her jewels. Even her fingers were bare.

"Why didn't you tell me you were here? I've talked with no one but the crew for weeks on end," Stelle lamented. Dr Moss was well aware of her status as a Lady, and it was required that he at least offer her some sort of society—although out here, it mattered little. That irked her. Stelle rested a hand on the pod, then immediately took it off.

"You didn't need to know. Besides, I hear you're getting along fine," Dr Moss said. His comment made Stelle blush, wondering exactly how much he had heard about her interactions with the crew. It was unladylike. She'd been raised better than to let herself fall so easily into society with a simple crew. She suppressed the urge to defend her actions; blame it on the loneliness. Then she remembered Dr Moss had been arrested and probably wasn't going to report her behaviour to her mother.

"What happened to her?" Stelle asked, looking down at the frozen pod holding Helen's body. The woman whose dresses she'd been wearing.

"She died," Dr Moss said dryly.

Stelle rolled her eyes and surveyed the row of empty beds. The size of the medical bay was almost as large as the one on the Monrovia.

A picture of the Lark formed in her mind—of its crew, and the dead woman, and now Dr Moss. She'd assumed the scrapper ship was hiding secret salvages or, at worst, smuggling. Never would she have suspected a hidden medical facility.

"Are you coming or not?" Dr Moss asked as he made his way down the hall.

Stelle trotted after him, keeping up with his long strides. When they reached the far end, a sitting area of sorts greeted them. The walls were an unappealing shade of blue, and the chairs were long, covered with soft white cushions. It was not an inviting place. Dr Moss poured himself a glass of haze, refraining from offering her one. He sat down and raised a brow when she took her time sitting across from him.

Without skirts to fuss with, she was at a loss. She clipped her heels together and turned them gently to the side. Lady Daye's stories of Dr Moss were always on the periphery of their conversation; she recalled bits and pieces that Lady Daye had told her over the years. Now she tried frantically to scoop them all together and make sense of the situation.

He waited for her to speak first. Stelle took her time. She knew Dr Moss had been involved in illegal medical experiments, but Stelle thought that was twenty years ago and that Dr Moss had abandoned that work.

"I thought Wynter was your last experiment. Is that what the Lark is? Are you trying to reverse the Idex coding again?"

Stelle asked. She hated to think of Merrick involved in such a horrible thing. She knew about the secret labs on Orion. Twenty years ago, when Wynter was born, Dr Moss had been the lead doctor who'd found frozen embryos from thousands of years ago, a time before the Idex. The lab was demolished, and Wynter was secretly stowed away on the Obsidian to work for a dressmaker. Lady Daye, one of Stelle's few friends, had requested she confirm Wynter was on the ship. Stelle had always known there was more to the story, but asking questions would have revealed Lady Daye's part in the plan to get Wynter onto Orion. And Lady Daye had her own secrets that Stelle had promised to keep.

Was Helen dead because of an experiment? Stelle shuddered trying to shake the creeping feeling of being on a ship where medical experiments were being conducted.

"No. That's not what the Lark is," Dr Moss said. He took a long drink. "Your Captain Merrick is a good man."

"And you're not?" Stelle asked.

"No. I'm not. But since you're here, I'll tell you all about your Valtine Idex."

Stelle's side ached, and she no longer wanted to ask him for a compress. Now that she knew it was Dr Moss, admitting she was in pain would be beneath her. She closed her eyes, not really wanting a lesson on the Idex, but knowing if she let him ramble on long enough, he might eventually tell her what she wanted to hear.

"What we call the Idex is actually an organic construct that is bonded to your DNA. It grows and replicates inside your body and gets passed down to your children—the same coding but mixed with their own particular DNA. The inventors, centuries ago, were the wealthy and the first to expand space travel and trade between planets. It was a way of tracking, and eventually ranking, everyone. What was once used as identification has become a parasite and means of control."

Stelle didn't like her Idex being referred to as a parasite, but she let him continue.

"So far, the bond between the Idex construct and our DNA has been unbreakable, and all attempts to separate them have caused a slow and painful death, which is why it's illegal. Ironically, over the centuries, the bond has weakened on its own. More satellites are required to transmit information, scans need to be more precise, and Valtine is losing its grip on the hex-system. It doesn't even bother with planets like Koros or space stations anymore."

The sound of approaching footsteps echoed down the hall. Her location had apparently been discovered, even without Idex tracking.

"How did you get in here?" Merrick asked.

Stelle pulled out the small card she'd lifted off Jasper and waved it in the air. Wincing at the pull in her side, she dropped the card and let it clatter to the floor.

"Dr Moss was going to tell me about why he was on the Lark. Won't you join us?" Stelle said sweetly, motioning to the seat beside her and trying to hide her discomfort.

"How are you?" Merrick asked, concern etched between his brows. Of course he would care more about how she was doing than about the fact that she'd snuck into the medical bay. Emotions warred within her. She wanted to bury her face against Merrick and pretend she was somewhere else entirely; she wanted to yell at him for not informing her of Dr Moss's presence; but most of all, she wanted to know what was going on.

"I'm fine," Stelle said. She could feel Dr Moss's half-hazed gaze, and a smile turned up at the corner of his mouth. Stelle pretended not to notice his clear enjoyment at her discomfort.

Merrick grabbed a compress from the ice bin. "Why didn't you tell me you were in pain again?" He sat down beside her, a little too close to keep her from blushing. She let him hold the compress to her side and braced herself for the initial cool sting before the flood of relief.

"The Lark's a rescue ship," Dr Moss said, breaking the tension in the room. "It's a salvage ship with regular work to fill, but with her speed, we can run two missions at the same time without detection. As you know, the Valtine court requires everyone to have an Idex and every system to follow a closely guarded set of rules. What you don't know is that the cracks in the system are growing. The Guilds have been trying for centuries to pull control from Valtine—in a peaceful sort of way. But there's a wave of unrest throughout the hex-system, and people are tired of waiting for the Guilds to grant them the smallest amount of freedom."

"But the Idex system keeps people safe. There wouldn't be space travel if not for the Idex tracking where everyone is," Stelle said, knowing she was spouting the same thing she'd heard her whole life. Saying it out loud while she was on an untracked ship—and after her life had been threatened multiple times—sounded a little silly.

"Your system is fragile. It relies on a technology that is slowly breaking down, both in terms of outdated technology as well as biology. These so-called medical labs are trying to exploit the weakness."

"But is reversing the Idex even possible?" Stelle asked. She couldn't help but wonder what life—what Valtine—would be like without it.

"No," Dr Moss said. "Not yet, anyway. If the Idex was being used only for safety, for tracking people when travelling, we wouldn't be in this mess. But I'm not working to help them reverse it either. It's too dangerous, and it doesn't work. That, and I don't care about your courts or your guilds or the ridiculous Idex problem."

Stelle waited for him to say what he did care about, but he fell silent. He opened a drawer in the side table. Four bottles of haze were lined up in a tidy row. He pulled one out, peeling off the seal like an orange. He let the curl of red wax fall to the floor. Uncorking it, he refilled his glass, then put the bottle back into the drawer. Merrick cleared his throat and continued where Dr Moss had left off.

"There are hundreds of young women *volunteering* for Idex reversal treatment. There are as many reasons as there are girls. Desperation and family debt. Some are promised a life on Valtine as a maid. Others, like Ava and her sister, are taken because no one will look for them. Idex doesn't mean much when no one cares where you are."

"Oh, don't hold back, Merrick," Dr Moss interjected. "On Valtine, when someone is too sickly or is a nuisance to society, they ship them off planet. Most of you higher-ups don't care where they end up, as long as the Idex is declared dead and you can continue to play perfection."

"As you've probably figured, Valtine wants every lab destroyed," Merrick continued, frowning at Dr Moss. "Like Dr

Moss said, we don't care about the labs or their work. We try to get the women out before Valtine, or anyone else, finds them. Ava has been with us for over two years. We had been working with Dr Moss, and after Orion we had a more difficult time getting messages to him. I'm not sure if you know this, but Dr Moss isn't his real name: it's a code we had been using to pick up information in various places. Jasper had a contact on Orion, and we saw an opportunity to talk to Dr Moss in person. We brought Ava and Helen with us. Then Dr Moss worked out a deal to join us. His absence won't be noticed."

Stelle knew why they had kept all this from her. But she should have noticed how ill Ava was. Her pale face, the comments about not being able to finish the book Stelle had bought her. She thought of the pod carrying Helen's body back home.

"How long does Ava have?" Stelle whispered, not sure she wanted to know the answer.

Twenty-Two

Stelle listened to Merrick and Dr Moss assault her with an overwhelming amount of information, trying to take it all in. Apparently, now that she knew the truth, they wanted her to understand. Part of her didn't want to. She wanted to go back to being annoyed with Lord Kent and his opinions on her jewels.

This was why civilized people didn't travel to the outer planets. It was nothing but kidnappings and attempted murder. Stelle heard the explanation as if it were coming from another world and tried not to focus on the one person she couldn't stop thinking about. Ava.

"Dr Moss has slowed down the progress, but Idex is connected to DNA in a way no one ever really understood—they just capitalized on it for generations." Merrick swallowed and ran his hand through his hair. "Ava doesn't have much time. Weeks…maybe a little longer. It's difficult to determine how much Dr Moss's treatment is working. Dr Moss has been working on this for years, and we've finally found something to help. There's no way yet to stop the process completely, but some might gain a year to two. I met with someone on Tornillo who gave us more information on another lab. There are so many more out there." Merrick's voice trailed off.

This was why Merrick had refused to bring her home when they first picked her up. The Lark and its crew had raced through the stars to find a cure, had bought time, and then had raced back to get Ava home again. Despite their efforts, Helen had died before the treatment could take effect, and either way, Ava was going to die as well. Without having to say it, Stelle knew why having a land-titled lady on the Lark was unfavourable—Valtine and the court she belonged to were the cause. She didn't have to be directly involved. She was a walking monument to the Idex system that had cost them their lives.

* * *

After packing up her belongings and returning to her own room, Stelle walked through the quiet ship, trying to regain her composure.

Stelle knew her perfect life on Valtine came at a cost—but she had always assumed she was the one paying it. Life on Valtine was pleasant and beautiful for most; but for her and ladies of similar rank, there were strict lessons and harsh treatment. Lack of food despite the feast in front of her. Never being able to mourn or cry. No emotions except the bursts of anger that had somehow been acceptable. Part of her wasn't surprised. She had witnessed enough secret exchanges and underground deals. Another part of her was crushed. For the first time, she understood why Jasper didn't want to use his title, because for the first time, she didn't want to use hers.

She was Lady Cristelle, heiress and titled. And despite the fact that she couldn't care less about her rank, it was the world she belonged in, the world she had to go back to.

Stelle knocked on Ava's door and let it slide open. At first she'd avoided Ava's room because she blamed herself for Ava being taken. Now that she knew what Ava had been through, she had to see her.

The room was dim. A soft glow light showed the disarray of clothing and towels. A cascade of bowls and cups littered the floor. Meals were being delivered, but no one had bothered to come in and remove the dishes.

She picked up a pile of clothing and tossed it into the bin by the door so she could reach Ava where she was curled up on her bed.

"Oh, don't clean up. I'll get it later," Ava pleaded. "You don't have to come in. I'm not very good company right now."

"Of all the people who are poor company to be around, your worst is probably my best. But do you need to be left alone?"

"I don't want to be a bother," the tiny voice said.

Stelle piled all the clothing into one of the laundry bags and stacked the dishes on a tray, then opened the door and pushed the mess into the hall, closing the door again quickly.

"I'm so sorry. I should have come to see you right away," Stelle said. She picked up a crumpled blanket and knelt onto the floor beside the bed. For the first time in her life, an apology came out of its own accord; for the first time in her life, she meant it.

"Don't! Please. What you did for me... I... I wouldn't have

done it for you." Ava's voice was hoarse, as if she had been torturing herself for the past day. Stelle wished she could go back a day and come to Ava right away, alleviating her concerns.

"I ran into Dr Moss," Stelle said, not knowing how to start the conversation.

Small tears formed in the corners of Ava's eyes. She blinked, and they slid down her cheek. Stelle brought the blanket up and wiped them away.

"Merrick thought it would be safer for us, and for you, if you didn't know. But I wanted to tell you. It felt wrong to say goodbye without you knowing." The words tumbled out of Ava, a stream of tears and memories. Stelle listened to her talk about the past—the Lark and the hope of finding a cure with Dr Moss. "My sister reacted as soon as they tried reversing her Idex. That happens sometimes. She died within a week. We didn't volunteer—my sister and I—there was just no one to come looking for us."

A deep rage spread through Stelle. She wanted to find anyone responsible for such a horrible thing and destroy them. She wanted to scream and throw things. Instead, she sat down on the floor and pushed a little pile of laundry that she'd missed under the bed.

"I have a sister, well I have four sisters, but only one close in age to me," Stelle said. She absently braided the wispy strands of hair and dabbed at the tears as they fell. "I would do anything to protect her and keep her safe. I'm so sorry."

Stelle sat in silence, unable to fill the void caused by so much pain.

Eventually, Ava's breathing evened out as she fell asleep.

Stelle rose from the floor, her feet cramped from sitting on them.

When she opened the door, the kitchen items were gone, and so was the laundry.

Twenty-Three

The Lark sped through space. Merrick worked in his shop and felt the weight of time as he willed the engines to move faster. Ruse's absence left an increase of work for Merrick, spreading his time thin. Aside from that, an intangible rift had opened between him and Stelle. She always waited until he'd made his way to the shop in the morning before she snuck into his unlocked rooms to use the shower. He cleared a shelf so she could leave her soaps, and neither said anything about the arrangement. He wasn't sure if the lack of communication with her was because of what had happened on Tornillo or because of the news about Ava and the Lark. She wandered the halls, deep in thought, and refused to look him in the eye.

She didn't tell him what she was thinking or feeling. He noticed that she stuck by Ava's side, and he knew she'd talked to Dr Moss more than once.

Merrick tossed aside the fried bit of tech. It rattled to the floor, and he thought of leaving it there. It wasn't as if he could learn anything new from it. He needed to see the detailed schematics of the Monrovia explosion.

When he emerged from his workshop, Jasper informed him of a scheme Ava and Stelle were working on. They wanted to have a ball—of sorts—on the Lark.

He couldn't stop it anymore than he could stop a hurricane. The next few days were a whirlwind of activity. They were less than a day from home, and Merrick had to admit it was a pleasant distraction for the entire crew.

Stelle convinced Merrick to set the lights to a twinkling glow and to hang lanterns from the ceiling. She had Lavalle slicing a large dress into long strands that she turned into flowers.

There was colour in Ava's cheeks, and she excitedly talked about the upcoming event.

The evening of the ball, Merrick put a soft recording of music through the whole of the ship's comms and set the lights to twinkle. The men were in various forms of polish. Merrick wore plain black pants and shirt. His dark hair was combed, but he'd forgotten to shave the shadow that crossed his jawline. Sers and Lavalle wore the same outfits they'd worn on Tornillo, except for the long scarves. Jasper refused to dress up, but at least attended. Dr Moss refused outright.

Stelle and Ava arrived and made a grand entrance. Ava's hair was braided like a golden crown atop her head; a string of Stelle's rubies hung around her neck. Ava lifted a gloved hand and touched the gems softly, then gave Merrick a smile.

His heart ached seeing her so happy. Merrick bowed slightly and raised Ava's gloved hand to kiss the inside of her wrist, giving her the formal greeting at a Valtine ball. Ava giggled and stepped aside as Stelle entered behind her.

Merrick half expected to see Stelle in the red gown she had arrived in. Instead, she wore a midnight-blue skirt with its edges gathered and tucked at the front, causing a wave. Flowers were pinned along the bottom, and matching ones danced along her neckline. It was simple but stunning, and Merrick could tell most of the evening's wardrobe efforts had been spent on Ava.

Merrick greeted Stelle in the same way. Her breathing was rapid, and when he raised her hand to kiss the inside of her wrist, he could feel her pulse. Kissing the air above her hand, his eyes locked on hers, and he wondered if he'd been the one avoiding her. She was confident and graceful and commanding. She stared back at him, then pulled her hand back in one swift movement, her breath catching.

She didn't look at him again while she effectively bossed everyone into two lines.

Jasper glared at Stelle as he bowed to Ava, and Stelle smiled sweetly at Sers, who stood across from her. Despite the emphatic protests, they all danced at Stelle's command.

Dr Moss poked his head into the room for a moment, and Ava kissed him on the cheek. He scowled, then went back to his side of the ship.

By the fourth song, Ava was exhausted. Merrick slowed the music and found himself toe-to-toe with Stelle. He hadn't planned it, but it probably appeared that way. Awareness ran through him as he put his hand around Stelle's waist and intertwined his other hand with her own. Stelle stiffened, and although she didn't falter in the well-known mechanical steps. He wished she would relax in his arms the way she had with Sers and Lavalle. When the music stopped, he released her. They abandoned the dance floor for the refreshments Sers had prepared. Once they were finished, Merrick thought the night might be over, but Stelle took Ava's old violin from its case. She cradled the beautiful instrument carefully, then set the bow to the strings. After a few slow songs, Stelle pulled a duet out of the box of sheet music and unpackaged the new violin she'd purchased for Ava on Tornillo, handing it to her excitedly.

The room fell into a hush as Stelle set the music onto the stand for them to share. If she was nervous it didn't show. She closed her eyes and listened for a moment as Ava set the pace, and then her absolute precision melded into Ava's tone. Ava stopped partway through, head bowed, tears falling from her eyes.

Stelle slowed, letting the bow rest.

Ava brushed the tears from her eyes. The words came out in barely a whisper. "I'm sorry, I've only ever played with my sister."

Stelle bit the side of her lip. "She was lucky to have you. I would love to be your sister."

"Some sisters happen at birth—I'd like to think others are found across the universe." Ava picked up the pages and put a new song on the stand.

"Sisters then?" Stelle asked.

"Sisters," Ava confirmed.

Sers tried to hide the single tear that trickled down his cheek as the next song filled the room. Lavalle elbowed him in the ribs, and Jasper's frown lessened a little. It wasn't simply a kind gesture. Stelle had announced to the room that she considered Ava family—an equal. Her shoulders were back, and a satisfied smile played at the corner of her mouth, confirming she knew exactly what she had just said.

Merrick calmed his features, afraid the entire room could see exactly what he had known for some time now—he was in love with Stelle.

Twenty-Four

The large blue planet of Koros glowed in front of them. The setting sun on the far side snuck a splinter of red light over the edge. Bits of light turned into a burst of colour as they made their way to the sunlit side of the planet. The crew were gathered on the bridge, strapped into their seats. Stelle experienced the full capabilities of the Lark as they pierced through the atmosphere.

She was used to the comfortable shuttle pods that brought passengers from the planets to the waiting ships. Never had she experienced a full-sized ship landing. White clouds melted into an endless sea. They passed over a series of low mountains and onto the plains on the far side. In the middle of the plains, they slowed. The Lark rumbled as thrusters brought them down toward the plain.

The Lark touched down on a long strip of grass. Fields rolled up and down. On the horizon, a mountain range kissed the sky.

Instead of the panic she expected to feel, she found she wanted to do the whole thing over again.

As soon as they landed, she ripped the straps off. Grabbing the bag she'd packed, unpacked, and repacked a dozen times in the past week, she sprinted down the hallway and waited for the hangar doors to open. Ava was close behind, wearing her best yellow sundress. Small flowers adorned her head in a circlet. Jasper joined them with three datapads tucked under his arm.

The door opened, and hot air swept up the lowering ramp to greet them. Real air. Fresh and muggy—not recycled air.

Stelle rushed past the others and onto the ramp. She paused midway, breathing in rapid gulps as if she were drowning. Jasper nudged her forward, and Ava skipped past them all.

When Merrick had said they'd stop at his shop before heading to the main house, she'd expected something small, not the grand building in front of her. On the other side of the Lark, a five-story glass dome rested among a cluster of tall trees. Red wildflowers burst from bushes and gathered in masses around the edge of the building.

A clear path wound its way toward the Lark's docking place, and a series of hover carts were approaching. Jasper was flicking his knife impatiently, and Ava circled around them, running her hands through the long grass that edged the runway.

Now that Stelle was outside the ship, she could see how large it actually was. It was a perfect twin ship with mirrored sides that could function independently. The sleek black design shimmered in the sunlight. A ripple of blue tech-light danced along the outer core.

Trying to take it all in, Stelle had never felt more out of place. She'd been avoiding Merrick, trying to suppress her growing feeling of comfort with him. She had prepared herself for a rough stay on Koros, and was unprepared for it to look so—perfect.

Stelle had lived with a tightness in her chest her whole life. It had slowly uncoiled during her time on the Lark. Now that they'd landed back on a planet, it coiled back up like a snake.

"What do you think?" Merrick asked, coming up beside her.

"I was thinking, if it wasn't for me, Ruse would be here with you instead." Stelle didn't know why Ruse had popped into her head at that moment. Because he would have fit in here—and she didn't.

"We should have pushed him out of an airlock," Ava said ruthlessly.

Stelle eyed Ava, wondering if this was another prank.

"But the shutters…" Stelle stopped, her attention fixed on the Lark and its unique design. It didn't have shutters covering the outer hull.

"Oh, it's possible," Jasper said.

"The Lark isn't like other cargo ships. It wouldn't be the first time someone suggested using the airlocks. They come in handy when we pick up unwanted guests." Merrick winked at her, and Ava gently punched him in the shoulder. Stelle watched as the dismembered parts of her safety pod were loaded onto large carts and hauled back to Merrick's shop.

A passenger trolley arrived, and they boarded. Stelle moved in her seat to accommodate Ava, who pressed on one side as Merrick joined them from the other.

"Sorry," Merrick said, noting her discomfort.

"I don't like being squished," Stelle replied. She stifled the urge to demand another trolly and turned her chin toward the sun. She knew it was only Ava and Merrick, but the tightness in her chest made her want to scream at being pressed in. Merrick put his arm over the back of the chair, giving her a bit more room, but the action made her extremely aware of how much closer they were without his broad shoulder between them.

The road was long and winding. A set of tracks ran parallel in the distance, then spliced from view behind a row of trees. They rolled along and shortly came to the edge of a small town. It was pretty, from what she could see. They crossed over a bridge. Tall glass buildings with walkways came into view. They turned and went down a side street.

Stone walls flanked a paved lane. Lanterns with swirling bulbs sat on top of twisting black and silver poles. As they crested a hill, a black stone house rose three stories high in front of them. The porch wrapped around the perimeter.

The trolley stopped. She noticed Merrick take a deep breath, as if preparing himself.

Jasper was already out, unloading and giving instructions before Stelle could move. Two well-armed men came out to help. The black butler-style uniforms couldn't hide the size of their muscles.

In the short ride over, Ava had fallen asleep, and Stelle pushed on her arm to wake her up.

Ava groaned, as if she was waking from hibernation instead of a five-minute nap. She rubbed her eyes and lifted a yellow-gloved hand to her mouth.

Stelle awkwardly nudged Ava with her hip.

Ava stood, and Merrick reached a hand to help Ava down.

"We made it," Ava said.

Merrick nodded. Ava pulled away from him and then, lifting the side of her skirt, went to take a step up the wide staircase.

The front door opened. A formidable-looking woman stepped out. She wore a black dress with lace around the hem. A corset cinched in her trim waist, and a navy apron covered the front of her skirts. A braid of white from the centre of her hair lay down on the left side and joined the dark black braid that hung over her shoulder.

"Ava!" the woman cried, ignoring the rest of the arriving party. She reached out to cup Ava's face in her hands and gently kissed each cheek before letting her go.

The woman tilted her head to the side, taking Stelle in.

Stelle recognized the look; it was the same one she always gave to unwanted guests at a ball. Stelle met her gaze, raised a brow, and smiled.

"I didn't realize you were bringing another one," the woman said to Merrick.

"We didn't," Jasper said, carrying luggage up the stairs. "Madame Dowswell, let me officially introduce you to Lady Cristelle." Jasper kissed the air above Madame Dowswell's cheek before entering the door behind her.

"Stelle," Merrick said, correcting the introduction. Taking her hand and bringing her up onto the porch, he continued. "I'd like you to meet Madame Dowswell."

"Madame," Stelle said in greeting, still refusing to drop her gaze.

Dowswell looked past Stelle to Merrick, waiting for a further explanation.

"You can put her in the third-floor valley suites. I'll explain later." He turned to direct someone who was carrying Ava's luggage.

Dowswell's face changed completely as Dr Moss neared. He had taken his own trolley and spent extra time loading up his medical supplies. He guided it toward the side of the house, jumped down, and bounded toward them.

He took the veranda stairs two at a time, lifted Dowswell up, spun in her a swift circle, then set her back down and gave her a swift and passionate kiss.

Then he did something entirely unexpected—he smiled. The corners of his mouth turned up. Stelle was certain it was a smile.

"Twenty years and still perfection," was all he said. Dowswell's sweet blush was quickly replaced by a perfectly calm expression as she playfully swatted him away.

Stelle closed her mouth, then looked to Jasper, who appeared equally surprised.

No one commented, and the business of moving everyone into the house continued.

The front hall was open and airy. Unlike the dark exterior, the inside was rosy. Pink and purple skylights tinged the surrounding air, casting shapes along the white walls. A pair of intricately carved white staircases flanked the main hall.

Feeling forgotten and slightly less significant, Stelle followed Dowswell.

It was strange walking into the house. She could tell by the doorframes that there were no Idex checkpoints. She had gotten used to the lack of Idex scans on the Lark, but she hadn't even considered a house without them. Merrick had explained that there weren't any Idex scans on this part of

Koros, but she still felt as though she was going to get caught sneaking around where she shouldn't. The tightness in her chest let go a little. Every movement wouldn't be tracked. She could move around freely.

They made their way up the stairs, ignoring the lift that was being loaded with luggage. Dowswell said very little, but looked back from time to time to make sure Stelle hadn't slowed her pace.

"We reserve the third floor for guests, not residents," Dowswell informed her. "Right now, it's only you and Merrick up here. Jasper and the boys will stay in the cottage. Dr Moss will likely stay in the medical wing."

Stelle smiled at Sers and Lavalle being referred to as the boys.

They reached the end of the hall. It opened up into a round sitting room, doors on each side.

Dowswell took a key out of her pocket and unlocked the door. Handing the silver key to Stelle, she opened the door and motioned for Stelle to follow her inside.

The room would be considered small compared to what Stelle was accustomed to on Valtine, but after months on the tiny ship, it was perfect.

There was a bed with soft white covers and light-blue pillows. White panelled walls, and decorative cove ceilings were edged with light blue trim.

"This door leads to the balcony. Keep your door locked when you are out. The other door is the powder room."

Stelle opened the veranda door, looking out toward the drive they'd arrived on. The warm air rushed in. There was a shuffle of noise in the hall, and the well-armed guards deposited her bags inside.

"Dinner will be at six," Dowswell said, motioning to the fantastic timepiece on the wall.

Once she was alone, Stelle lined up all the lotions and bottles in the bathroom, then took a long soak in the tub.

There was a rack waiting outside her room with four dresses hanging on it. She chose a rose gown with cropped sleeves and a beaded edge. It would be more comfortable in the heat than the pants.

She curled her hair and put on a hint of blush.

Adding a few jewels, she felt like herself again, armoured against whatever the outer planets were going to throw at her.

It was shortly after six when Stelle finally left her room. The kitchens were on the main floor and should be easy enough to locate. Stelle strode through the empty halls to the dining room. A spindle chandelier hung over the lace-covered table.

Side warmers were empty, as was each seat.

The soft ring of music floated through open windows. Stelle walked through the adjoining kitchen. It was bustling with people, laughing and arranging platters. Double doors were open to the veranda behind the house, and Stelle followed the swell of people outside.

The whole town must have heard that the Lark had returned. There were tables and food being brought out and set up.

Movement in the line of trees near the border of the stone wall caught her attention, and she watched two guards walk the perimeter. Dowswell was in the centre of the crowd; like a conductor, she directed the flow of food and chairs.

Ava was in the distance, stretched out in a lounge chair

under a tree and surrounded by a group of women. A blanket hung around her shoulders, and another one covered her feet.

Stelle didn't want to intrude on the moment. Ava had known the girls for some time, and Stelle didn't belong. She wasn't even sure how to introduce herself.

Turning from the party, she made her way around the veranda.

Stelle sat on one of the white wicker chairs, arranging her skirts so they fell softly to the side; she waited for the pounding in her chest to settle.

She was on a planet. Her feet were on land. She should feel better, more at rest. She was off the small ship. But somehow this all seemed worse. This longing—an ache deep in her chest for Valtine—was a longing for home. The moment she let the longing take over, this dream of the perfect world she'd grown up in, the tightness twisted and pulled.

At least when she'd been on the Lark, they were moving. Now she was stuck here, far away from everything. Not moving. The inability to change her fate—to go back, to make her own choices—strangled her.

"There you are." Merrick came around the house. A plate piled with food was balanced between his hands. He sat down in the chair beside her and put the plate on the decorative table between them.

"You were looking for me?" Stelle asked, her heart lightening up.

"Wanted to make sure you settled in." He stretched his legs out in front of him.

"I don't like it here," she said, trying to not sound hopeless.

"You didn't like the Lark at first either."

"That's not true."

"I'm sure you'll feel better once you join the party." The noise from the other end of the house was growing. She was ignoring the people walking past her.

The sun sank quickly, revealing three moons spread across the sky.

Merrick waited patiently, then eventually stood and held out his hand. Stelle took it, and a spark passed between them.

Fires were being lit as they returned to the back of the house. She stepped closer as they crackled and popped and then jumped at the sound of musicians starting up a song.

She was unsure without the rules, without the formality of it all. Merrick stayed by her side, and her feet itched to move to the music.

"I know it's not where you want to be, but these people are great if you give them the chance."

"What if they won't give me a chance?" she said, unable to shake the feeling she didn't belong.

"What? The infamous Lady Cristelle afraid of what the outer planets might think of her?" he teased.

"Never," she said, grabbing his hand, and pulled him onto the lawn, determined not to care.

Twenty-Five

Merrick let himself relax. They had one evening to enjoy before their next mission. The information he'd received in Barrons on Tornillo was sound. There was a confirmed lab on a small, uninhabited planet only a few hours by dart. They had schematics, floor plans, and hopefully accurate information— as accurate as it could be for months old.

The stars twinkled above, and a breeze cooled the dancers. Stelle danced most of the evening with him but also accepted offers from a few of the other men. As the evening progressed, he watched something in Stelle let go. One of her dance partners said something that caused her to laugh. Merrick had seen Stelle smile, be amused, chuckle even. He had never seen her laugh. Her face looked as if it had broken out of a perfect mould. She had been coolly beautiful. But this? His heart twisted, and he wondered if he had ever seen anyone more beautiful. Her cheeks raised in a stunning smile as she grabbed her sides to control the laughter. With a swipe of her hand, she cleared the moisture from her eyes, then kept right on dancing.

When she declared her feet too sore to continue, she came back to his side, near a long row of lounge chairs pressed together like matchsticks.

Stelle sat in one of the lounge chairs, leaning back. Where another woman might look sprawled, she looked as though every loose strand of dark hair was exactly where she wanted it to be. Her skirts fluttered over the side, the hem disappearing into the dewy grass.

"I won't say it was better than a ball," Stelle said, and then yawned as he passed her a cup of steaming hot chocolate from the tray that came around.

"We stay up till dawn," Merrick said. "Every time we make it back, we stay up and watch the sunrise. You don't have to stay up with us."

"You prefer I go to bed?" Stelle asked tartly.

"No, I like it when you're around," he said.

Stelle wrinkled her nose and glared as if she were facing down a firing squad and not merely receiving an unsolicited compliment. He wanted to pull her in closer, to tuck the moon-kissed hair behind her ear.

She blinked and looked up at him under dark lashes.

Before he could dwell on what she might be thinking, Ava and her friends bombarded them, sitting down on either side and squeezing more and more people into the long row. Ava wanted to know what Stelle thought about everything. The girls wanted grand stories about Merrick's adventures. Soon they were crowded beyond capacity.

Merrick moved closer to Stelle, half straddling the bump where two of the lounge chairs squeezed together and shifting to keep from spilling his hot chocolate.

Stelle pulled her skirts up so they weren't being crushed and stiffly settled into the crook of his arm. Ava and the girls giggled and talked.

A hush settled over the group as the surrounding air lightened. The lower moons glowed red along the horizon. Then a strip of sun danced through the trees and over the fields.

Sunrise.

Stelle grabbed Merrick's hand, her breath catching. He waited for a moment for her to pull away. When she didn't, his hand closed over hers and held it. They sat motionless, suspended in the morning light.

Once the rays of pink and gold finally melted into the morning, the group pushed themselves up from their chairs. Stelle released his hand only long enough for him to stand, and when he offered it again to help her up, she didn't let go. They trailed everyone back into the house and walked up the stairs to the third floor together. Merrick was sure the thundering of his own heart could be heard over the soft fall of their feet on the carpets. When they reached the end of the hall, he raised her hand, turned it over, and placed a kiss on the inside of her wrist. Her eyes wide, she searched his face. She didn't back away immediately but also didn't move toward him.

He waited a moment longer, wishing he could share his feelings, but tomorrow they would follow up on the information they'd received on Tornillo. Tomorrow they would walk into danger—again. He was walking into an unknown situation, and after that he would have to make plans to take Stelle home—where she belonged.

Merrick slept restlessly. Thoughts of Stelle filled his waking moments as well as his dreams. He slept in through most of the morning and into the early afternoon, knowing he needed sleep for what they would be facing.

He made his way down to the dining room, grabbing an odd assortment of breakfast and dinner foods, and then joined Dowswell. She poured him a cup of steaming coffee.

She wore black, as usual, her hair tied back in her customary braid. "You said you were going to explain," Dowswell said, nodding to where Stelle sat looking out a window in the adjoining parlour. She had a book open on her lap, more to ward off attention than to read.

Merrick sipped the strong black spiced coffee. Explaining Stelle would be a difficult task. How could he simplify everything that had happened over the past weeks in space?

Dowswell patted his hand. "She must have done something special to make you look at her like that, unless you're taken in by her ladyship's charms."

Something special. Everything about her was special. From the first moment, when she'd charged out of the safety pod after what must have been a terrifying ordeal, only to demand cortivals… to the handcrafted dresses she was so proud of… to her friendship with Ava. And then there was the way she played the violin—like her heart was bleeding on the strings.

"We're leaving soon. I hope to only be gone a few days. I'm sure you can manage one lady."

Dowswell took a sip of her tea and settled the flowered cup back into the saucer. "I could manage a hundred ladies; it doesn't mean I want to."

Merrick looked back to where Stelle was sitting, eyeing

everyone over the top of her book until Ava entered.

Ava was carrying two violins. Stelle put down her book, and the girls disappeared into a side room. After a few testing notes, music floated into the kitchens.

"Ava's playing again?" Dowswell said, surprised.

Merrick nodded. Ava was playing again. Merrick didn't hide his feelings for Stelle as he detailed the events—from picking her up, to Tornillo, the poisoned tea, Ruse, and the ball.

"I'll keep an eye on her," Dowswell assured him and patted his hand once more before getting up. Merrick knew it wasn't just a promise for the following day. It was a promise she'd keep even if he didn't make it back.

Twenty-Six

The dead planet was uninhabited. Charred remains of vegetation littered the side of the mountain before it rose to sheer rock. The dormant volcanic landscape made the planet a poor choice for anything—anything except a secret medical lab. The Lark was too large to navigate the narrow canyons, so they'd travelled in one of the smaller darts. The dart hovered behind a mountain range, avoiding detection from the medical lab.

"Look Sers, another not-so-secret, secret lab," Lavalle said.

"At least this one fits in with the landscape," said Sers. "We need our own secret lab."

"We are far too busy, busy, busy to sit around in a lab doing nothing."

Merrick gave them a glare, suggesting this was not the time for jokes.

The stealthy craft slid through the mountain range, staying as close to the jagged edges as possible.

The facility jutted out from the base of the cliff, a long landing pad marking its location. Parachutes tightened, Jasper nodded to Merrick, who opened the side door. The wind pulled and whipped past them, shaking the dart. As they shot over the lab, Merrick and Jasper jumped from the dart, free falling to the left of the landing pad below.

Every second in the sky felt like minutes. Focused on his target, Merrick tucked his arms and turned slightly. Once they were in range, they pulled their chutes, slowing their descent to the landing area.

The chutes closed when their feet hit land, and they quickly made their way around the side to where a small opening was. Hot and muggy air smelled like thick, burning sulphur as they walked the nearly abandoned halls.

Merrick had memorized the floor plans. The tunnels led to dorms down one hall, a lab in the centre, and living quarters for staff on the far side.

They reached the dorms first, hoping the girls would be alone and easy to sneak out. Unfortunately, six beds in a row were all empty. Littered around the rooms were opened trunks, blankets, small stacks of books, and a few personal items. Merrick felt guilty leaving any of it behind. These girls had packed up everything they had to come here, knowing years of freedom would be taken away. They'd probably never expected to be tucked away on some unbearable planet.

The mountain rumbled, and loosening debris rained bits of dirt down on them. Jasper raised his hand.

A voice down the hall made them both pause. Jasper stilled the double blades he'd been spinning between his fingers.

"Tremors and shakes—how am I supposed to conduct these experiments working in these conditions?"

"We're safer here," another voice echoed.

"I thought that's what the guards were for," the first voice said. Merrick mouthed the word *guards* to Jasper, who just shrugged.

The voices retreated, along with the shuffling feet. By Merrick's estimation, they were unfortunately headed toward the medical bay, where they would likely find what they were looking for. Around the corner, Merrick spied two guards outside the door to the medical lab. There was no sign of more. Merrick stepped to the side as two blades flashed like lightning through the air, dropping both guards.

Jasper collected his blades as they entered the lab, quickly assessing the situation. The lab was in a deplorable state. The instruments were in bowls of antiseptic, and tubes were hanging from the ceiling. Evenly spaced reclining chairs lined the far wall. Five women sat up. They all wore grey pants and tops. Mesh caps covered their hair. One screamed, then covered her mouth with her hands. Merrick surveyed the room, seeing no sign of the doctors.

The girls weren't restrained. It wasn't as if they could get far on the desolate planet. Merrick carefully unhooked the monitors, handing each of them the adjoining datapad to carry out, hoping the information would help Dr Moss. He spoke softly but urgently, making sure they could stand and walk.

The door to the right of the room opened. Two doctors stumbled out with shouts and calls for the guards. One man sprinted for the door, the other just stood stunned for a moment.

Jasper's attention divided; he flung a blade down the hall, then turned, loosing another.

In a flash, Merrick saw what Jasper hadn't. The doctor

grabbed the closest girl, using her as a shield. Merrick jumped in front of the blade, and it sunk deep into his shoulder.

Shock registered on Jasper's face, then he loosed another, this time hitting his target.

Weakened, Merrick fell to one knee. Blood ran from the wound and soaked his shirt. Jasper swore, grabbed the bottom of Merrick's shirt, and ripped it open. He tied it over his shoulder, holding the blade in tight.

There wasn't an objection from the women as they silently herded them down the hall. If there were more guards, they were either too far away or had run.

"They talked about you—" said the tallest, and probably oldest, of the girls. She had fiery red hair that poked out from under the cap and a string of bird tattoos that flew up her arm. Her big, brown eyes stared at Merrick. She looked at the trail of blood seeping through the tied-up shirt and slid her arm under his other shoulder so he could lean on her for support. He wanted to protest, but weakness gripped him. "The guards were all afraid. We heard them whispering about you. We knew the ghost ship would come."

Merrick swallowed. Renown wasn't something he wanted the Lark to have. It made things dangerous. How many more labs had the rumours offered hope to? Labs they would never be able to reach.

From the small medical bay, they headed toward the tunnel that would bring them to the landing pad.

"There should be one more girl," Merrick said, counting the five who were walking well enough. Six beds. There should be one more. The woman who was helping him led them down a side hall, leaned him against the door, and nodded to Jasper.

Jasper opened the door. He took a minute to look inside, then called the all-clear. Not a sound came from the isolated room.

Merrick leaned around the frame to see inside.

There was a gurney in the middle of the narrow room. A cart sat abandoned with some medical supplies and discarded notes on top. A girl lay unmoving on the bed. If she was breathing, there was no sign.

Jasper reached the bed. A deep rage flashed over his well-controlled features. Without unplugging everything, he placed the pile of wires and tubes as well as the datapad on her chest, then lifted the small girl into his arms. She couldn't be a day over ten years old.

Merrick's heart constricted as Jasper brushed past him, looking straight ahead as he carried her out of the room toward the landing pad.

The hot sulphuric air poured in through the side of the mountain. Merrick faltered as they reached the dart. Sers was there in a flash, helping the girls in. He didn't comment on the blade sticking out of Merrick's shoulder. Jasper stepped in next, still carrying the wisp of a girl. Merrick pulled himself through the door and closed it. They sat side by side, squeezed into the small space.

"She has a pulse," Jasper said, cradling the almost lifeless body.

They all huddled, cramped and half on top of each other in the dart as it took off. Merrick wished he had words to tell them everything was going to be okay, but he had lost too much blood. It dripped down his side, making his body weak and his eyes heavy. He closed them as the dart exited the atmosphere and darkness took over.

* * *

Stelle paced back and forth on the veranda. The lilac bushes gave off a heady scent. Bees flew in and out around the flowers, shaking the petals as they landed. She hated that she was watching bees, waiting for Merrick. He had been vague when he left. She should have asked more questions, demanded that he give her details. But this was what they did—what they were all out there for.

The ship finally arrived. It hovered high over the grand house lawn, making the grass swim and the trees bend. The dart landed where they had been dancing only days ago.

As soon as it landed, guards with float gurneys flanked by Dr Moss and Dowswell sped towards the dart. Stelle hadn't been given a job. No one told her she should help. She didn't know what to expect but raced toward the craft anyway.

The door opened. Two of the women came out of the cramped space, stumbling forward as Dowswell passed one to Stelle's waiting arms. The smell of medicine and rot overwhelmed her, and she fought the urge to wretch.

The girl looked up at the sky, the half moons large and glowing pink behind the sun. Dirty blond hair plastered the side of her face, and tears soaked her cheeks.

"Come along, we'll get you a hot bath and something to eat," Stelle said. Whatever had been coiled in her chest for the past day splintered. She didn't know what these women had experienced. She didn't need to.

This was what drove Merrick to take a titled lady across the known universe. He was right. He had always been right. The mission they had been on was more important than any titled lady and her demands.

Stelle walked beside the young girl, whose eyes darted with disbelief around them. When Stelle looked back, Jasper had disembarked. A lifeless body in his arms was placed on a gurney. Dr Moss focused his attention on the girl and began barking orders. And then Stelle saw Merrick. Lavalle dragged him from the dart. His torn shirt was soaked in blood and wrapped over one shoulder. Even from a distance, she could distinguish one of Jasper's blades protruding from Merrick's shoulder.

She wanted to run to him, but couldn't abandon the girl who leaned on her arm. They made their way toward Dr Moss's wing of the manor. There was a flurry of activity as they neared, Dowswell was giving instructions, and everyone was moving at once. Merrick was white as they wheeled him past her. Holding her breath, she kept herself together, waiting for him to pass.

"Sorry," Jasper said, coming up beside her. He looked suddenly younger, more helpless, and she wanted to reach out and hug him, give him some comfort. Jasper ran a hand through the long black hair that flowed down to his shoulders.

It was the first time she'd seen him with it down like this. He looked slightly less dangerous with the waves of black onyx framing his frown.

"I'm sorry," he said again. Stelle wasn't sure if he was apologizing to her, or to Merrick, or to no one in particular. She rested her hand on his arm, gave it a gentle squeeze, and resisted the urge to demand he relinquish every last blade he was still carrying.

Twenty-Seven

Stelle did not have a free minute to worry about Merrick. They promptly informed her that he was fine and stitched up, and that would have to satisfy her. Compared to the young girl Jasper had brought in, Merrick's injury was of little concern. The girl, however, almost died multiple times. Jasper didn't leave her side, and when she finally pulled through, the whole house breathed a sigh of relief.

Like hosting a grand event on Valtine, the same level of activity hit the house. Stelle helped in setting up rooms, making tea, and walking the girls to and from Dr Moss. Despite Dr Moss's intelligence, he lacked the ability to carry out his duties with anything resembling empathy. After Stelle had to bring the red-haired girl back in tears, she decided it was best to sit with them. She countered Dr Moss's sour words and softened his mood.

In the main house, the constant activity continued. The dining room was perpetually filled with food: tarts and sweets, meats and cheeses, grapes and berries and spicy dishes that rivalled the work of her Valtine chef. There was comfort—

often tears—and the sharing of stories as the girls sewed gowns and embroidered tops. Stelle wandered among the group, picking at the food and encouraging bits of conversation, offering an occasional hug.

Merrick recovered well, but his mood was altered. He was more driven, talking about the next mission despite Dr Moss's insistence that he couldn't go anymore. Stelle became even more awkward around him. His conversation was clipped and tired. The only person he wanted to talk to was Sers. When he was finally released, he took off to his shop, murmuring about the next problem to fix.

Stelle sat on her veranda after he left, finally able to take a break. She hid behind a book all afternoon until Ava joined her. There were moments when she felt comfortable and at home, and other moments where the distance between her and Valtine was so vast she couldn't breathe.

The evening closed with violin playing, solo this time, as Ava retired early. When the lights on the main floor dimmed, Stelle made her way to bed, the loneliness of the third floor wrapped around her.

Nightmares shattered the day's monotony. First she was in her safety pod, the walls crushing her as the oxygen depleted. Then she was on Tornillo, except it was abandoned and empty. Stelle woke in a cold sweat, her throat raw and aching. Taking a long drink from the glass of water beside the bed, her fingers trembled. Instead of immediately forgetting, this nightmare clung to her like the sheet tangled around her legs.

The edges of her nightgown threaded between her fingers, and she clutched them and tumbled out of bed. She opened the veranda window to let in a cool breeze and calmed her breathing, but even the night air couldn't stop the overwhelming memories. It was cruel of her mind to create something worse than reality.

Closing the shutters, she paced again and rubbed her arms, wishing she could scream at the unfairness of it. It took her a moment to realize it wasn't the comfort of Valtine she was longing for. She wanted the sway of the ship, the sounds and smells she'd gotten used to. She wanted the Lark, and the man who captained it.

Giving up hope of finding comfort in her own room, she opened her door and peeked her head into the dark hall. Barely lit wall lanterns cast dancing shadows up and down the inky tunnel. She snuck across the hallway. Merrick was staying at his shop and wouldn't be returning for at least another day. She let out a sigh of relief as the door opened silently. Moonlight lit the room, and she crept in and crawled into Merrick's empty bed. Breathing in the familiar scent, she curled up under his blankets, hoping he wouldn't be back early to catch her, and drifted back to sleep.

Morning leaked through the open curtains. Stelle cursed herself for forgetting to close them and remembered she was in Merrick's room, not her own.

For the first time she was thankful that she didn't have servants seeing to her morning routine as she made her way back to her room. The shower was extra long, and she dressed in a mint-coloured gown; long laces down the side cinched in at her waist. The hem was knee length and ruffled in a full bloom around her legs.

As she made her way downstairs, she ran her hand across

the intricately carved wood bannister and followed the sound of laughter and noise.

Stelle spied Ava sitting in a chair overlooking the gardens. The other women circled around her, hanging on her every word.

Stelle had been afraid of a nightmare; Ava was living it. The happiness in her smile didn't hide the sunken cheeks and shallow breathing. With each day that passed, the hope of Dr Moss being able to cure her slowly faded.

Ava's voice carried through the room and reached her ears. "…she wears her jewels everywhere, even to bed."

The girls snickered and giggled. Stelle's face flamed. Something twisted in her stomach, probably the effect of an awful night's sleep.

Stelle took a few long strides, pretending she hadn't heard, and entered the room. Ava brightened when she saw Stelle and motioned her forward.

"I was telling them all about you," Ava said. She took the smallest bite from a biscuit. Little crumbs tumbled down into the folds of the rose blanket.

"Are you really from Valtine?" one of the younger girls asked, blue eyes wide. Her reddish-blond curls bounced.

"Are there real lords who dance with you?" Another girl pressed up beside her.

Stelle held her smile perfectly calm. Inside she was a hurricane of emotions. Each one of these girls had sold themselves—or had been sold by someone—as an experiment for a war she didn't even know she was a part of. Each one faced the same fate as Ava if Dr Moss couldn't find a solution. Stelle wanted to take them all home to Valtine—to what end, she wasn't yet sure.

"Let's give Stelle some space," Dowswell declared, sweeping into the room. A crimson apron adorned her usual black dress. White pinstripes ran up the edges and hid a pocket. "Stelle, help me make the tea."

It was unladylike to make tea for such a large gathering, but Stelle was thankful for this distraction.

Through the large stone archway, she found her way easily in the kitchen. Aqua paint trimmed soft-brown cupboards with shiny brass pulls.

Stelle lifted the canister out to make the tea. The pot was a similar contraption to the one on the ship, except larger.

"Do you know how to use that?" Dowswell asked as she wheeled a cart to the cupboard and loaded it with fancy mugs.

"Merrick has a smaller version on the Lark," Stelle said, trying to hide the blush that rose to her cheeks at the mention of his name.

"Of course he does," Dowswell replied.

"Your accent isn't like the rest," Stelle stated, focusing on the pot. She was trying to not outright ask about her greeting with Dr Moss. She hadn't seen them together since.

"Merrick helped me find a friend a few years ago," she replied.

"So you are from Valtine?" Stelle guessed, knowing the accent was not Valtine. Even the northern islands didn't roll their r's like she did.

"Corva," Dowswell replied.

Stelle wrinkled her nose. She'd always disliked the stops on Corva. The dancing was fast and the gentlemen fussy, and as long as you could afford a decent dress, you could attend a ball.

Dowswell ignored Stelle's clear dislike for her home-world and piled a plate with more biscuits. Stelle wanted to mention that the first ones hadn't been eaten yet, but held back.

"I'm glad Ava is playing the violin again," Dowswell said.

Stelle nodded, calm and ready to face the swarm of young girls. As soon as she'd poured the tea, they peppered her with questions about Valtine. Stelle told story after story about balls and parties and dresses. She had a never-ending supply of tales about her sister, Violet, and the lengths to which she'd go to keep her out of trouble. There were even more stories about her and Lucy. Ava sighed and closed her eyes as if she was imagining it all.

If Dr Moss's treatments worked, Stelle swore she would bring Ava home. If Dr Moss's treatments didn't work, then she had to do something for the remaining girls. Plus the possible hundreds more who hadn't been rescued.

An idea started to form in her mind. Stelle wanted to bring all of them home. As the girls left the sitting room, some went out back to sit in the sun. Ava drifted off to sleep in the chair, and Stelle got up. She wanted to talk to Merrick, to tell him her plan—or at least the beginning of her plan.

The front veranda swept down into a garden and curved around to a long line of trollies. Stelle eyed the silver machines, then set out on foot past bushes bursting with red and pink roses. A tall arch stretched over the driveway; blue morning glories burst from the vines. It hadn't taken that long by trolley to get from his shop to the house. The walk couldn't be more than an hour or two at the most.

The guards didn't give her a second glance, and no one

stopped her as she marched out of the gated estate and back through the town.

Passing the last home, she spied the tracks and walked beside them. She knew as long as she kept them to her left and the mountain range in front of her, she'd be fine.

Clouds puffed up over the mountains. It was hot, and she wished for the big, tall columns to reach her way and cover her from the sun. But they were playing their own game as they peeked over the mountain, promising shade, only to shrink back into themselves and hide behind the mountain range.

After the first hour, a soothing wind picked up and blew her hair. The breeze turned against her, and the uptick of dust stung her eyes.

The air warmed. The sweet smell of damp grass and lilacs swirled around her as the air cooled, then warmed, then cooled again.

She looked over her shoulder, hoping to catch one final look at the village, but the rolling fields and forest blocked it from view. In front of her were endless fields—and the track she'd been following. She had to be closer to the ship than to the village. There was no point in turning back now.

Her feet ached; a bead of sweat poured down her back. Stelle removed her shoes and swung them between her fingers as Merrick's shop came into view.

* * *

Merrick came around the corner and stopped short, taking in the sight of Stelle in his shop. Her hair tumbled over her shoulders in a half-braided mess. Dust covered her from head to toe, and she looked as though she'd been playing in a sandbox. Back straight, she handed her dusty shoes to the nearest person. Despite her appearance, her eyes were bright.

"I had an idea, and now that I'm here, I realize it was an impossible thought. I can't bring the girls to Valtine." Merrick had no idea what she was talking about, but she looked so defeated. She looked around the large workspace. Half a dozen men were working on her safety pod. They'd reduced it to scrap and unrecognizable bits. She absently picked up a coil of wire from his workbench. Merrick felt bad he hadn't been there for her these past few days, but time was limited, and his injury had put him behind.

"I'm sorry I've been so miserable—you didn't need to see me like that. Honestly, I don't take well to Dr Moss's medication. I healed fast, but it always comes at a cost."

"Don't be silly. We all have bad days."

"Unfortunately, I'm going to make yours worse. Do you want to sit down?" Merrick suggested. He wished there was time to figure out how to tell her this. Merrick raked his fingers through his hair, then looked down at the datapad. Stelle leaned over, not the least bit put out by his concern. The others in the shop had all stopped working and were listening intently to the exchange. Merrick lowered his voice and leaned in toward her.

"Home might not be the best idea right now. It might be very dangerous," Merrick said, then took a deep breath.

She waited for him to continue, raised a brow when he didn't, and wiped her dust-covered hands on her green dress.

"Your safety pod was equipped with a unique release that I couldn't figure out," Merrick began. "Once I received the

Monrovia reports, I confirmed that the safety pod actually caused the explosion. I'd suspected the cloaking technology had caused the blow back into the ship—but now we know. The pod was set to release to your Idex."

"Are you saying—I caused the explosion?"

"It was never meant to cause an explosion. Someone rigged the safety pod to release once you were inside. What they didn't count on was the cloaking technology—it kept the safety field from engaging. Without the safety field, the blowback from the safety pod ejection caused the explosion. Don't you remember anything?"

She paced the floor, flexing her hands, then shaking them slightly.

"I was checking on the perfumery cargo. I do that every few days. Someone came up behind me. I don't know. It was all so fast. There was an alarm, and they pushed me in—or the alarm sounded afterward. I thought they saved me. You're telling me they messed up? That I was supposed to be sent off in the safety pod and no one would have even known I was gone?"

"Someone paid a lot of money to make you disappear without a trace. The cost of something like this… it's out of even Lord Terrington's scope. If you go back—"

Merrick grabbed Stelle's trembling hand and held it. He wanted to tell her she was welcome on Koros, or even back on the Lark. That he would keep her safe, and find a way to fix this.

Stelle pulled her hand back from his. Without another word, she ran from his shop.

Twenty-Eight

The facade crumbled. Bits had been picked away over the years, and irreparable cracks had formed long before the Monrovia. Valtine, with all its pleasures and beauty, hid a sinister darkness. Someone wanted her dead—enough to send her off into space to die alone in a safety pod. How long could she have survived there? And they had unintentionally killed five other people in the process.

Stelle pulled away from Merrick and bolted from the shop. The muggy air surrounded her as she ran. The tightness in her chest squeezed until it felt like her lungs were going to burst.

Her aching feet sent a sting of pain up her legs with each step, but she needed to get away. Away from her safety pod and away from Merrick. She gasped for breath, hands on her knees, and regretted running so far.

Thick clouds heralded a curtain of rain.

It swept over the mountains and covered the large peaks. The previously puffy clouds turned black and were unleashing their torrent on the ground.

"Come on, then," Stelle yelled at the storm as it swept

toward her. "Do your worst!"

The storm answered back with fat drops of rain that soaked the green scarf and dripped down her face. Within seconds, the rain had soaked Stelle through. The wind picked up and battered against her, like tiny thorns catching the side of her dress. She covered her eyes with her hands, trying to blink through the driving rain, unsure if she was moving forward or simply walking in place.

Stelle screamed at the storm, throwing her fists at her side. She was Lady Cristelle and would not let a storm defeat her. The storm roared back, engulfing her in a wave of water and wind.

Lightning struck, shimmering through the rain. Stelle counted, waiting for the boom that eventually followed. Trying to get a bearing, she knew she wasn't in a field and that the trees were about the right distance away. Her foot slid a little in the forming mud as another bolt of lightning struck much closer.

Hands over her head, Stelle screamed in surrender, calling out for someone to hear her. And then screamed again as a trolly scooped up beside her.

Merrick wrapped an arm around her waist and lifted her onto the seat in front of him. The wind tried to pull her away, as if it was going to lift her right off the seat.

As they neared the Lark, the trolley threw them off as it skidded and slipped in the mud. Ankle deep, they walked the short distance to the Lark. She held onto his arm, trying to not pull him down as she slid. Rain dripped from her lashes and into her eyes, making it impossible to see.

Merrick's arm reached under her and pulled her toward the

ship as the side door opened. A spray of water rushed into the opening with them.

Stelle collapsed onto the floor as the door closed behind them, shutting out the wind and noise. Merrick lay on the floor beside her, soaked from rain and covered in a splattering of mud. He rolled onto his side and shook the water from his hair. As he stood, slops of mud splattered onto the floor. He reached down to help her up, but her foot slid in the muck, forcing her to grab tightly onto his arms.

"Stop saving me," Stelle said through chattering teeth. Her heart thundered in her chest as he helped her to her feet. The pitter of her dripping dress made a muddy puddle on the floor at her feet. Her hair hung in strings and stuck to her cheek.

Stelle's breath caught as she looked up at him. He focused his gaze on hers, unleashing butterflies in her stomach.

"You're the only one who doesn't need saving," Merrick said. He pulled a bit of hair from her cheek and wiped the mud off with the side of his hand. His fingers traced her jaw, moving behind her ear and then to the back of her neck.

Stelle closed her eyes. All the pain and fear of the last few months melted as he closed the space between them. Lightning struck as his lips found hers, sending electricity through her whole body. She pulled herself closer, grabbed on to his wet shirt and pressed herself up against him.

The storm raged outside. She reached up, ran her fingers through his hair. She tried to move closer, but her foot slid on the slick floor. A scream escaped as she put both hands on his chest, barely keeping her footing.

"Don't look so horrified," he said as he steadied her. He reached up and pulled a bit of soggy hair away from her cheek.

"It's okay to enjoy being kissed by a common salvage captain."

He was teasing her, again. She studied his dark eyes, and the slight creases at the edge when he smiled. He held her to keep her from falling, waiting for her to make the next move. He was a salvage captain, and she would eventually return to her life on Valtine. But in that moment, all of the reasons why she shouldn't like being kissed by Merrick washed away with the rain.

"We both know you're not common," she replied and then kissed him again.

Twenty-Nine

Stelle was eager to talk to Ava. She wanted to tell her everything and could imagine the shocked look on Ava's face when she heard that Merrick had kissed her. Perhaps she'd be even more surprised that he hadn't kissed her again. Instead, they'd dried off, showered, changed, and watched the storm from the Lark's bridge.

Merrick didn't bring up the issues with the safety pod again. She wanted to forget the problems that lay ahead. Stelle listened to the pelting rain, wondering what life would be like if she stayed on Koros—if she could find a family with Dowswell and Ava and the other girls. Wondering who she would be if she wasn't *Lady* Cristelle. Dawn broke, exposing the extent of the storm's damage. Trees were bent and large pools of water covered parts of the track. The raised road was mostly clear aside from branches and debris that littered the area.

Merrick cleaned off the small trolley, inspecting it for damage; then they rode together back to the village.

Stelle rushed into the house. No one was in the kitchen, and since it was early morning, she guessed Ava would more likely be in her room than outside. The storm had probably kept half of them up during the night. Stelle brushed past Dowswell, who was making her way down the hall. She called for Stelle to stop, but Stelle barely heard her.

She took the stairs two at a time, smiling with each step. She never would have rushed to tell anyone anything; how much her world had changed in such a short time.

Ava's door was open. Dr Moss was leaving and looked startled when she flew past him, paying him no mind.

Closed curtains let in a small stream of light that picked up the slightest hint of dust; it glittered from the window pane down to the floor.

Ava was in her bed, her face still as she slept.

Stelle frowned at Dr Moss. He certainly shouldn't be there if Ava was sleeping. She almost called out to him, but then she noticed how still Ava was.

Stelle knelt down beside her. Ava was always pale and a little frail looking, but she was different now.

Stelle grabbed her chilly hand in hers and immediately dropped it back down.

Taking the blanket with soft lavender flowers etched around the edges, she covered Ava's icy hand. She held onto it, waiting for Ava to wake up, to move, to breathe.

"Stelle, you shouldn't be in here," Dowswell said. She was by her side, gently pulling at her arm.

There was a commotion in the hall as news spread through the house. She knew she was crying and could feel the hot tears rolling down her cheeks.

"Stelle, dear, you need to come away."

Everyone in this house had more reason to be sad than she

did. But like the wave of the rain, her body felt pressed to the floor. The anchor of grief had its chains on her heart, pulling her down.

"Come away, Stelle," Merrick said from the door. He knelt down beside her, then pulled her away from the bed. She wanted to kick and scream, but all fight had left her.

She let Merrick guide her out of the room, up the stairs. Her legs buckled as they reached the end of the hall. Merrick caught her as she sank to the floor. He wrapped his arms around her, holding her still. She leaned against his chest, listening to his heart beating.

Merrick's eyes had been bright in the morning and now looked sunken with sadness. They cried together until there were no tears left.

* * *

The funeral took place the following day. A sea of black mourning dresses paraded around the back lawn, the hems of their skirts soaking up the damp grass.

They would do this for the day, then bury Ava together at nightfall, along with Helen, whose pod was also being laid to rest. They would spend a week in mourning.

Stelle had never attended something so beautiful and crushing at the same time. On Valtine, they wouldn't have done anything. Sadness was not a pleasant emotion, and everyone carried on as if nothing had happened. Death was an ugly part of life no one talked about there.

On Koros, they embraced sadness.

They gathered, ate, and drank, like the first night on Koros watching the sunrise.

Arrival and departure—all celebration. Except no one was celebrating.

Tears flowed freely and small groups talked in hushed tones. Stelle wanted the solitude of her room, but didn't want to be alone.

Tea pots on a side table were empty or missing, and so Stelle made her way through the arched doorway back into the kitchen.

There were full pots waiting, but she wasn't ready to go back out. She slowly dumped the perfectly good tea down the copper drain, and set out to make new ones.

When Dowswell joined her in the kitchen, Stelle expected a command to stop. Instead, Dowswell helped run the water and thanked Stelle for remaking it.

"How do you do it? How do you say goodbye to them, one after the other?" Stelle asked, inspecting the lines beside Dowswell's eyes. They made her look older. They were lines from laughter but also from constant tears.

"It's what I've been called to," Dowswell replied simply.

"I can't do it," Stelle said, reminded of her earlier plans to bring the girls home with her. Dowswell put a hand on hers.

Dr Moss stumbled into the kitchen, breaking the women apart. He looked worse than usual. Stelle stepped back and pressed her back against the wall. Dowswell led him to a chair and put pressure on his shoulders, forcing him to sit. She filled a cup of tea, stirred in two sugars, and placed it in front of him.

Dr Moss took a sip, then with a swipe of his hand, set the teacup and plate flying across the room. It hit the wall and shattered, spraying tea across the linen tablecloth and white walls.

Merrick rushed into the kitchen. Dowswell held up her hand and just shook her head.

"Ah, good—Captain—I was looking for you," Dr Moss slurred. He blinked slowly, then patted the pockets of his jacket. When he found what he was looking for, he pulled it out and set it on the table. A scrap of paper and a black vial. "Your cure."

Everyone in the room held their breath, waiting for Dr Moss to continue. He waved his hand at Dowswell, who folded her arms across her chest.

"If you want it, you'll have to stand and get it yourself," she replied to his gesture.

Stelle wasn't sure he could stand. The chair scraped across the floor. Dr Moss stumbled to the cupboard, uncorked a bottle of haze, and took a long drink. The counter held half his weight as he closed the lid and, almost dropping the bottle, passed it to Dowswell, who set it carefully on the counter.

"When Ava died, I analyzed the final breakdown of the Idex on her cells. I have your cure."

The room fell silent. Stelle knew there was more Dr Moss wasn't saying—but there was always more Dr Moss wasn't saying. A strange knot formed in Stelle's chest. The sadness, the wrongness of a cure coming from the death of her friend. The rightness of a cure coming from her dear friend. And anger swirling around it all.

"We have hope?" Dowswell whispered. She let out a strangled sob and covered her mouth with the back of her hand.

"What about justice?" Stelle asked, knowing it wasn't the right time.

"Justice is Jasper's business," Merrick said. He reached across the table to pick up the vial and scribbled notes.

As if he could sense they were talking about him, Jasper walked into the room. He looked even more dark in the black suit with red trim, with the flickering blade in his hands. He was the only one who didn't show signs of tears. He frowned at Dr Moss and nodded in Merrick's direction.

"We have enough tea," he said, then spied Stelle. "The girls are looking for you. They want you to play for Ava."

Stelle stood, stunned, until Jasper placed the violin in her hands. How could she play for Ava? She wanted to say no, to run. Instead of running away, she took the violin from Jasper and followed him into the gardens as the sun set.

The women stood around the casket as they lowered it into the ground. Stelle wondered if they knew—if Dr Moss had told them they wouldn't be following their friend to the grave. The tallow candles they held flickered against the sunset.

Stelle pulled the bow across the strings and then played a lament as she mourned the death of her friend.

Thirty

Seventeen days after Ava's funeral, the Lark was reloaded and prepared for its next excursion. The entire village came to see them off.

Stelle wore a long gown with a black travelling coat. Bits of lace and feathers trimmed her hair. She'd accumulated eight trunks stuffed full of new clothing. The steel blue clasps with wind-cogs strained against their contents. She'd sold two of the rings to pay for everything, which Merrick assured her was unnecessary. But she was happy to leave the Valtine jewels behind. Stelle was pushing on a trunk lid as Dr Moss stumbled up the ramp.

Stelle was aware that Dowswell had tried to convince Dr Moss to stay—as had Sers and Lavalle—but Dr Moss was adamant that he would return to Orion, back to the prison everyone assumed he still occupied.

A cure wasn't enough; he had to help get it out there, and he couldn't do that from Koros.

After delivering him to Orion, Jasper and Merrick would meet up with a contact on a small moonbase near Corva.

"I still don't understand why you won't stay here," Stelle said to Dr Moss.

"The prison follows me," Dr Moss replied, a slight wobble in his step. "Doesn't matter if I'm here or there. If I'm there, then there's more to be done. Besides, I could ask you the same question. You're going to spend the next hundred days flying on a salvage ship you can't get off of."

Stelle pretended she didn't hear him. She had no place, either on the Lark, on Koros, or even on Valtine at this point. Jasper had another contact on Orion, and there was hope they could locate who had been commissioned for the tech used on her safety pod. If they could track that, then they might be able to find out who had attempted to kill her.

She abandoned her trunks and walked past him down the ramp to say her last goodbyes.

Stelle hugged each of the girls tightly and wiped away a nonexistent tear.

Sers and Lavalle, despite their general ease and relaxed moods, perpetually talked about being ready to go back to work. They marched up the ramp, matching beige pants, Lavalle topped in red and Sers in black.

Lavalle lifted one of Stelle's trunks. "You know what, Sers? Everyone here has two good hands between them, and you know who ends up doing all the lifting?"

"Us," replied Sers, grabbing the other trunk.

Merrick was the last to join them. He held out his hand to escort Stelle onto the ship and didn't let it go as they made their way to the bridge.

In mere minutes the Lark rose through the atmosphere, and they were back among the stars.

Stelle made coffee and enjoyed long showers in the mornings. She spent her days with Sers and Lavalle on the bridge, or visiting with Dr Moss when he would put up with her. She sat with Merrick in his shop and watched from the higher decks as they retrieved salvage.

They stopped four times, and she always enjoyed the thrill of wondering what it was they would pick up next. The process of matching velocities, then scanning and loading items was not a fast one, although they did it with smooth precision. Scrapping lacked the refinement of the perfumery business, but the surprising complexity of it drew her in. He often pulled little wires and nuts out of the panels and would mutter at vials of blue-gold liquid as he carried bits to his shop.

They stayed up late into the evening when they were weary from work and needing rest. Stelle and Merrick sat together on the small chaise, her legs draped over his. He'd hold her hand, and they would talk.

Merrick kissed her three more times. Each time he did, Stelle wanted the moment to last forever, knowing it would all end too soon. Even in his embrace, she couldn't forget she was from Valtine. Her family thought her dead, and she had to return home.

The more days that passed, the less Stelle wanted it to end. She wanted to be a part of it, wanted to help. But she had no idea how. There was nothing she had to offer, nothing she could do to help.

In an attempt to distract herself, Stelle made her way to Dr

Moss. He was leaning over a small vial of blood, datapad resting to the side. He clenched his jaw and stretched, flexing his muscles before inputting his findings.

"What do you want?" he asked.

"I just came to visit. I noticed how well you and Dowswell got along," Stelle said daringly. She wasn't sure why she thought to ask about Dowswell, but it should be a reasonably safe subject.

"Why?" Dr Moss tucked the instruments into a locked cupboard and poured himself a drink. "Never mind why—I need a break anyway."

Sitting in the uncomfortable lounge, Stelle waited as Dr Moss took a long drink. She tried not to think of Tornillo, when she was forced to drink the rotten, poisoned sludge.

"I don't mind you, Stelle. You're curious about Dowswell, and with no concern for my feelings or anyone else's, you just go ahead and ask."

It stung like an insult, but Dr Moss was handing it out like a compliment. She wasn't sure she wanted a compliment from Dr Moss.

"No one else has bothered to ask about Dowswell; there's not much to tell. We were both young when I first met her twenty-something years ago. We've kept up correspondence once or twice a year."

"Why didn't you stay? With her?" Stelle asked, wanting to reach over and hold his hand. He looked old, not in age, but in time. He must have blamed himself, but there was little Stelle had experienced that she didn't blame herself for causing either.

"There are so many secrets. Which one do you want? Are

you curious because you want to fill your own need for stories?” In that moment, in the way he leaned forward, he looked dark and dangerous.

“I thought you might need a friend. Ava taught me that we all do.” Dr Moss’s face crumbled at the mention of Ava.

“I started all of this,” he began. “Every single woman who has died from these experiments is because of the work I did. Don’t look at me with pity. I don’t deserve it.”

“Surely you didn’t intend for any of this to happen.”

“I did. We were going to find a way out.”

“We?”

“The woman who gave birth to Wynter was my wife.” The declaration came out as if he were saying that he liked his coffee warm. Stelle closed her mouth, and she was very uncomfortable. He continued in the same manner.

“She came from the outer planets and travelled to Orion to join the medical guild. She wanted to bring medicines back to her home. Her Idex wasn’t good enough, and when they escorted her off the campus for the third time, I knew I’d met my future wife. I met with her in secret and taught her everything I was learning. I married her. We found the lab and a group and funding and started our research. We were going to reverse the Idex. It was her idea to experiment with the frozen embryos. She didn’t survive the delivery, which had nothing to do with the Idex.”

Stelle sat in silence, wishing she knew what to say.

“I never told Wynter. She would have concluded there was some sort of connection to me.”

Stelle thought it useless to inform Dr Moss that Wynter clearly already had a strong connection with him, whether or not he liked it, so she held that in.

"What if we just stopped using the Idex?" Stelle said, surprising herself. But all this talk of medical labs and experiments was aggravating. The solution was so simple and yet so impossible.

"And what? Went with the Guild law? Sorry to break it to you, but guild law is just as tied to the Idex as the Valtine Court."

"What if we stopped caring? What if we just refused—oh, I don't know. How do we stop this?" Stelle asked, feeling frustrated and defeated.

Dr Moss held up his drink in a mock toast and drank the contents in one long swig.

Thirty-One

Stelle stood on the bridge, nervous about their next adventure. They'd returned Dr Moss to his prison Orion and then reached the lunar base near Corva.

Lunar bases were not appropriate places for ladies to socialize. They were more of a destination for those with the funds to do something, but not so extravagant as to travel between planets.

The Lark docked on one of the hundreds of towers. The long silver tube elevator ran down to the base. Stelle was disappointed she had never come here before, and that she wouldn't be able to go down with them now. The moonbase was more of a village. From where she stood, she could see glowing blue stones that lined the white stone walkways. The rooftops of shops and cafes stretched close to the top of the dome, open to the view of the stars.

Despite the seriousness of the situation, she struggled to control a laugh when Merrick and Jasper joined her on the bridge. Merrick wore an older-style Corvan scarf. They had decked it in fast trims, and the fabric swept down toward the floor. He was clean shaven—something Stelle hadn't seen since Ava had died—and smelled a little too strongly of pine and lemon. Jasper's dark-red shoes were shiny, but the rest of his outfit looked worn, with a hint of flare around his collar. They looked like merchants who were trying to appear wealthier than they actually were. It was an impressive transformation.

"This is just a regular meet up," Merrick reminded her. "If they don't show, we move along. We have news of the cure, and hopefully they have new information for us. This won't be like last time."

"Won't you be scanned? Your Idex?" Stelle asked. She hated having to stay on the Lark simply because her dead Idex would—well, no one knew what it would do.

"The only scan point is at the entry, just like one of your fancy balls. We all have our own ways of getting around the intense controls. And believe it or not, the Lark is a fully licensed salvage ship. They expect my Idex here."

"And Jasper?"

"He left Valtine behind, and no one is looking for him. The only concern is if he shows up in too many places too fast," Sers explained.

"I have a chart." Lavalle waved the datapad in the air to reassure her.

"I wish I could do something," Stelle said. She didn't like that they were going down to the moonbase, but they reassured her so many times that there was nothing to worry about.

Merrick tugged at the sparkling jewels on his cuffs. "If anything goes wrong, for any reason, the Lark needs to leave without us."

The bridge held silent for a moment except for the almost imperceptible flick of Jasper's knife.

"Well, let's get moving," Jasper said, breaking the tension and moving towards the door.

"Wait," Stelle called. Her plum dress swished as she stood. Her heart was beating quickly. She was so afraid for Merrick, not so much for Jasper. Reaching out, she grabbed Merrick's hand but didn't know what to do with it.

Jasper leaned impatiently against the door frame. Stelle hated having an audience. She wanted to tell Merrick how she felt, but the words stuck. After weeks of being told the dangers of what they did, she hated having him out of sight. She didn't want to lose him. Something grabbed at her, wanting her to say a hundred things she had never told anyone.

"It's just information, Stelle. You don't have to worry," Merrick said, squeezing her hand tightly and misreading her stalling.

"People kill for information," Stelle replied.

Jasper groaned.

Merrick raised her hand in his; turning it wrist up, he kissed the inside of her wrist. Her heart fluttered, and she took a step back. When he released her hand, the cool air rushed between them. Stelle held her wrist, waited for the door to close, and didn't dare turn around to face Lavalle and Sers, who were wisely quiet.

Everything was perfectly clear now. She knew why the Lark felt suddenly empty now that Merrick was gone.

She had lost it.

Somewhere between the stars, she had lost her heart, and she would never be able to get it back.

Thirty-Two

Merrick and Jasper walked from the Lark into the transparent tube and took the lift down to the moon.

In the centre of town, a brewhouse rose four stories high. The outside was copper, with a rounded front window and second-level patios. Jasper walked the perimeter as Merrick entered. The room smelled heavily of hops and spices. Glistening tubes of amber-and-gold liquid ran over the bar and down to the taps. Blue-and-grey crystal decanters holding haze lined the back walls, along with something purple Merrick didn't recognize.

Merrick chose a black leather seat toward the front of the dining area so he could watch the street and the brewhouse interior at the same time. He checked his timepiece and waited.

Instead of his usual contact, though, it was Ruse who took the seat across from him. Although he'd cut his hair unfashionably short and wore a typical shuttle uniform, Ruse hadn't attempted to disguise himself. Merrick swore to himself and tried to keep his voice as passive as possible. The crew of the Lark had barely entertained the idea of Ruse actually causing any trouble. He was, after all, on their side of things. They had changed codes and scrubbed any information that Ruse could use against them. He'd forgotten that Ruse was with them long enough to know about this planned stop at the base.

"It's probably too much to hope that you have information for us," Merrick said dryly, trying to hide the frustration in his voice. Four other men sat down with them at the table, giving Ruse a nod. With any luck, Jasper had seen Ruse enter and had enough time to warn their contact. If so, Jasper would already be gone, taking the Lark and Stelle with him. Merrick assessed the problem in front of him, wondering what Ruse could possibly get out of the exchange.

A round of drinks arrived at the table. The waitress was abrupt and clearly annoyed that there were more patrons than she had expected. Ruse took his time, waiting for the waitress to leave.

"If you're hoping Jasper is gone, I have a man on him. He isn't going to warn the Lark away," Ruse said smugly. "I know your next move. You were always consistent. At the first sign of trouble, the Lark takes off. Except you didn't take off from Tornillo, did you? You chose Stelle over everyone you swore to protect."

"Careful with your words," Merrick's eyes narrowed, keeping his voice low. To an observer, they would appear to be having a friendly talk.

"Still defending her. You should have left her on the satellite. I did what you were too weak to do." Ruse took a long drink from his curved mug and slammed it down on the table.

"I'm not sure what I can give you," Merrick said. He gently leaned back in his chair, trying to look calm and draw out the time they had.

"I want the Lark," Ruse said and mirrored Merrick's posture. Merrick hid his shocked expression. There was no way Ruse could handle a ship like the Lark.

"The Lark isn't mine to give. You won't get her going without Sers and Lavalle."

"I don't need them. I have my own pilots. And we're going to do whatever it takes to end this," Ruse said, nodding to the men at the table beside him. Merrick stared in disbelief. Not only did Ruse underestimate the skill Sers and Lavalle had, he also underestimated Lavalle's uncanny attention to worst-case scenarios. He'd built redundancies into the Lark, in the event it should ever fall into the wrong hands. Not only that, the men who were with Ruse looked less convinced of the rightness of Ruse's mission, and more intrigued with the Lark.

"Well, clearly you've outmanoeuvred us. Why don't you tell me how you want the rest of this to go? I suppose you want to negotiate," Merrick said. He hoped Jasper had made it back to the Lark and doubted anyone would have been able to follow him.

"I don't think you understand. You left me on Tornillo to die—"

"Hardly—" Merrick watched Ruse closely. His weapon wasn't obvious, and there was no way he planned to kill Merrick in the brewery.

"I'm not going to leave you and Jasper alive to hunt me down. You've done an excellent job of staying hidden—no one is going to miss you."

"If you think four men are enough, you've clearly miscalculated," Merrick said. He evaluated the problem before him, playing through all the possible ways this could end. Incarceration was most likely. Taking another long drink—and hoping Jasper was gone—he wondered if he would ever see Stelle again.

Thirty-Three

"But how long do we have to wait?" Stelle asked again.

Jasper and Merrick had been gone far too long. Stelle had taken the time to pull out a deep-red gown. Layered skirts folded over each other and belled out. Little crystals and black stones accented the tight waistband. Coal-coloured laces ran up the back and over her shoulders. Her arms were bare, but matching gloves hid her fingers. It was excessive, but she felt as if everyone saw her feelings for Merrick, and she needed to hide within the layers.

Stelle ran her finger across the navy arm of the chair, picking at the pulls for the belts.

"Why don't you go make us some tea?" Sers said, not turning her way.

"Excuse me?" Stelle said, no longer intrigued by the plush chair.

"You cork," Lavalle said to Sers. "Don't go asking her to make you tea. Remember what happened last time?"

"I thought it would get her out of here," Sers shrugged.

"I am not making tea for you. I'm not some sort of—" Her

words were cut short by a soft ping sound in the control room. "What's that?"

Lavalle and Sers both jumped into action, and the side hatch opened.

"Finally!" Stelle cried but stopped short. Jasper came in, hair dishevelled and missing his scarf. He didn't even glance in her direction but went to a small panel on the far wall. He typed in a code and a door sprang open, revealing a row of long blades. He flung off his long coat, tossing it over the chair Stelle had been sitting in and slung a holder over his shoulder. Small blades danced up his arm, one on his leg.

"The second I step out this door, the Lark needs to take off," Jasper said.

Lavalle was already at the controls.

"What's happening?" Panic rose in her chest, and her hands shook. Where was Merrick?

"Ruse didn't appreciate being left on Tornillo." Jasper laced up new shoes and slipped a final blade into the side, then straightened and faced Stelle.

"Ruse isn't playing. He wants Merrick dead, and he wants the Lark. I'm going back for Merrick, I can keep him alive but we'll likely get picked up. But this way, if things don't go as planned, Ruse won't take the Lark. Nice knowing you. Lavalle —Sers—it's been an honour." Jasper offered a half-bow to the co-pilots as if they hadn't spent every spare minute of their journey teasing him.

"Wait!" Stelle grabbed Jasper's arm. Her mind was racing. She bit the inside of her lip. She wanted to stay, wanted to never leave the Lark. But what was the point if Merrick wasn't on it anymore? "The moment I step through the main arch, my Idex will be scanned. I'll be the only thing anyone is interested in. No one will care about whatever it is you plan to do until you're long gone. This is all my fault anyway,"

Jasper stopped. Lavalle's hand rested over the controls.

"If I alert the authorities, you'll have a distraction, it'll give you enough time to get Merrick out."

"We don't have time—" Jasper started.

"No. You don't have time. The Lark needs to leave, and it needs to have Merrick on it," Stelle said decisively.

"You can't come back," Lavalle said. All three men were staring at her.

"We all know I never belonged here," Stelle shrugged, tears misting in her eyes. "Looks like I won't be making any more tea."

Jasper stared at her a moment, thoughts flickering across his face. Part of her didn't want him to agree to this plan. She wasn't ready to say goodbye.

"It won't be safe for you to return home, we never figured out who was trying to kill you."

"Everyone is, apparently. Tell Merrick goodbye." She quickly kissed Sers and Lavalle on the cheek, squared her shoulders, and motioned for Jasper to lead the way.

They exited the Lark and stood on the small docking pad. The door closed behind them.

Stelle let Jasper get a head start, and time for the Lark to disengage. Time for Sers to pilot the dart that would pick them up.

At the bottom of the elevator, she stepped out and through the arch. An alarm would have sounded somewhere or recorded something. Jasper had told her where to stop—close enough to cause a commotion, but far enough away to keep the attention fixed on her.

She thought she spied Jasper out of the corner of her eye but didn't dare double check.

Stelle walked down the white stone road as if nothing was wrong. Red skirts fluttered, and gem-toed shoes glittered under the halo lights.

It didn't take long for the wind of whispers to scuttle through the streets. By now, her connection with the Monrovia would be circulating. She wondered if Merrick was already gone. If the Lark was on its way.

"Umm, Miss?" A portly man with a dozen tasselled scarves approached her. Guards lined the streets, unsure of what to do.

"*Miss?* Do you know who I am?" Her tone sounded foreign to her, her brain fought against the name she'd buried down. "I am Lady Cristelle—and I demand someone take me to the embassy."

* * *

The movement of a security team walking past the brewery caught Merrick's eye. Ruse paid no mind and continued to explain how he had talked the four men into working with him. He wanted Merrick to understand why he thought him unworthy of the Lark.

"I told them there was a ship that could take us anywhere in half the time," Ruse said. Merrick never knew Ruse could talk so much. He bided his time, waiting for the commotion outside to grab Ruse's attention. The moment Ruse looked out the window Merrick took advantage of the brief distraction and pushed away from the table. He tipped the chair backwards to slide into the aisle and move toward the exit.

Before Merrick got far, Ruse was behind him with a blade, pressing it into Merrick's side.

"I don't—" Ruse's words were cut off. He clutched his throat, a blade protruding from his neck. The other four men looked around frantically to see where it had come from.

Merrick already knew. Jasper hadn't left on the Lark.

He used their momentary confusion to pick up the chair and take out the man closest to him. The next came to his companion's aid but fell where he was with a blade in the back of his leg. The final two turned and fled, clearly not as committed as Ruse.

"The Lark was supposed to leave at the first sign of trouble," Merrick stated.

"You're welcome. Let's go!"

They ran into the street and slowed their pace. He bumped into someone as the crowd pressed in the other direction. Merrick wondered for a second what could have drawn so much attention.

"Is she really alive?" someone asked. Guards were flooding the street, and patrons looked out the balcony windows.

Merrick stopped dead. Jasper slowed.

"What is going on?" Merrick demanded.

"It was her idea, and I couldn't see any other way that didn't end up with you dead or both of us incarcerated for a really long time," replied Jasper. "Sers is waiting with the dart."

Merrick hesitated, but Jasper grabbed his arm and dragged

him down an alley.

"We need to get out of here, or have you forgotten about the dead bodies we left behind?" whispered Jasper.

Merrick looked back and reluctantly followed Jasper to the rendezvous point. They boarded, and took off before Merrick could stop them. As they swept away from the base, Merrick stared at the growing crowd. They were gathered around a woman wearing a fiery red gown.

Thirty-Four

Stelle was quickly transferred to Corva, where she waited for an acceptable ship to bring her back to Valtine. After the initial shock of the Idex system malfunction, everyone was just thankful when she left. Her presence had caused the system to set off an unknown alarm. It was confused and overloaded and would perpetually reset. Which was fine until she walked through another scan.

The constant attention left her dizzy and frustrated. It was a week of soft beds and maids who brought her food and tea and haze, which she pretended to drink but dumped down the sink. They pinned her hair too tight, and wanted her skirts too full —and they wanted to talk.

They all wanted the story and pretended to help to catch little snippets of gossip in the hall. Stelle played it off exceptionally well. She was good at this part, she reminded herself. Tales of being overwrought circulated. There was no way she would ever tell the truth; instead she let the mismatched stories slip out. Each day, a wilder idea came to her, and she shared the smallest bits with anyone who would listen.

Rescued by pirates was her favourite. The majority believed she'd spent a month on a luxury outer planet with spas and mountains and hadn't even thought of home or the family who mourned her. Returned whispers about her family's lack of mourning flitted around with the rest. This didn't surprise Stelle. She was from Valtine, after all.

Some thought she must have lost her memory. Who could know what terrible things might have happened to her?

All of them were good stories. Little bits that everyone was trying to piece together.

Stelle wove a web that would have everyone focusing on all the wrong things. Relief finally hit when she boarded the ship to take her to Valtine. It was smaller than the Obsidian, but at least there was a pool. She demanded the captain skip the midway and press on.

His face went pale, and he stammered a good deal, but with the return of a Monrovia survivor—how could he say no? He had cargo and other passengers to think of—Stelle thought it rather pathetic that he didn't say no.

Upon their arrival at Valtine, she landed on Lady Daye's estates instead of her own. There was a ball in a few days, and her family would be here instead of one of their own homes.

When she mentioned attending the ball, there was a hush and whisper that she couldn't quite catch. It made her uneasy, but perhaps that was partly due to Jasper's final warning about someone wanting to kill her. Whoever it was, they would not be happy to hear she was alive.

Lady Cristelle walked up the white marbled stairs. The moons circling Valtine cast shadows on the water. She paused for a moment, looking out and then up to the stars above.

She was home, but it didn't feel the same. Like part of her had been buried with Ava on Koros, part of her remained with Merrick, and bits of her heart were on the Lark. She was splintered and yet more whole than she ever had been in her entire life.

She ran her hand across the cold white pillar that held the Idex scans. Her location logged and noted, probably setting off an alarm somewhere in the house. She wondered why an Idex had ever made her think she was better than anyone else.

She let the Idex come up on the guard's datapad and noted the confused look on his face.

"Is there a problem?" Stelle asked, then remembered she shouldn't have addressed him directly. As she stepped past him, another attendant met her in the hall.

"Lady Cristelle, if you'll excuse me, we don't have your rooms made up. We didn't know you'd come *here*."

"That's fine," she said and waved her hand in the air. "I'm sure it won't take long—"

"It's not—it's—well, you were… not here… and we…"

Stelle walked past him. She didn't care which room she stayed in; she needed a room, any room.

The white walls of the airy hall were suffocatingly tight, as if they squeezed out every breath from her lungs. She couldn't do this. She couldn't walk back into this life. Taking long strides, she flew up a flight of stairs and down another hallway, where she usually stayed when visiting Lady Daye. The attendant who was following her was joined by two others. She needed to get away from all of them.

A door opened, and before Stelle could stop herself, she ran full speed into the lady walking through it.

"Lucy!" Stelle cried. Stelle hadn't even considered that Lucy might be there. Relief and dread flooded her at once. She'd expected Lucy to be on Orion, not at a ball on Valtine. Although a lot could have changed in the time she'd been gone.

Lucy let out an unladylike squeal and clasped her hand.

"Lady Cristelle?" she gasped. "But what are you doing here?"

The attendants paused a discreet distance away. Stelle glared at them.

"Apparently, I have no room to stay in," Stelle said dryly.

"Well, of course you don't. You are dead, you know." Lucy looked past Stelle and called to them, "You'll move Lady Claire out of my adjoining room—she's so dull—and prepare for Lady Cristelle."

Stelle wanted to tell her it was not only unnecessary but also not very kind to Lady Claire, but she held her tongue. She wasn't going to change Valtine overnight. The attendants hesitated. Lucy elbowed Stelle in the ribs, and she straightened and shot them a glare that sent them all running. Lucy pulled her into her room and closed the door.

The room smelled like citrus and sweet candies. Lucy had gowns draped over every surface and tossed a pile of them aside to make room for Stelle. Pink and green and something in deep rose crumpled to the floor. Lucy pushed them with her toe until they were out of the way.

"I'd let you stay here—but I don't have any room." Lucy smiled, her blue eyes dancing. "I'm so thankful you're here. You know, ever since Aunt Daye vanished and you—well, we thought you were dead. I heard you were alive, but I didn't believe it. Oh, wait till everyone sees you! And my uncle has been keeping me on this dreadful planet. I have no idea why he insists I stay. Aunt Daye is missing, and they keep telling me it'll be ten years or a body before I can take over my aunt's lands. Which everyone is talking about because of course you didn't have a body… well you have a body, but it's still intact."

Stelle reached over and hugged Lucy tightly and clung to her.

"I missed you," Stelle said, then released her. Picking up a berry from the plate on the table, she popped it into her mouth and flopped onto the couch, relishing the surprised look on Lucy's face.

"What did your family say?" Lucy asked.

"I haven't seen them yet. I just arrived." Stelle got up as abruptly as she'd sat down and began opening cupboards, looking for a pot to make tea. She was restless and agitated.

"You came here first?" Lucy made no move to help Stelle with her search, but concern etched her brow.

"I heard there was to be a ball. I assumed my family would be in attendance."

"Well, yes—they arrive tomorrow. I'm acting hostess. I didn't want to be. I thought of making it a miserable event, but my uncle threatened me. The ball is for Violet."

"Violet? My sister?" Stelle hadn't even thought to ask what the ball was for, which would be why no one wanted to talk about it.

"She is being officially presented as heiress."

Stelle closed the decorative white cupboard and rested her head against it. She had been declared dead, and months had passed. With her mother alive, there was no rush; but of course they would host a ball.

Stelle hadn't even considered losing her status as an heiress. She'd always assumed she had years to work with the Inkton shipments and travel before she was a titled landowner. Aside from a small portion set aside for her sisters, most of the estate was hers.

"But you're back! Which means this party will be a grand welcome home party!"

Stelle didn't share Lucy's shiny outlook. Her family might be pleased she was alive, but changing a ball would be a disaster in their social circles. Could she walk away from it, allow Violet to inherit?

The thought was a dizzying one.

"I suppose whatever will happen will happen," Stelle said dismissively and finally found a tea pot tucked away on a top shelf. She rinsed it out and filled it with water, then set it to boil.

"I could call for tea," Lucy said.

"I'd rather do it myself. Tell me, what has it been like for you?"

"Dreadfully boring. I've been trying to find any clue of what happened to my Aunt Daye. Since she disappeared, there's been nothing but meetings and ambassadors and old people from all over who want to talk about meetings. The guilds had a deal with Aunt Daye. It was supposed to go through next year, but with her gone, they're unsure if I can take her place. What do I know of guilds? There's talk they murdered her because of the meetings, or because of some summit." Lucy's voice got quiet.

The swirl of steam rose from the delicate china teacup as Stelle poured the water into it, remembering her last interaction with Lady Daye at the ball on Orion. "I'm sure wherever your aunt is, she's perfectly safe."

"Do you know something? I knew you two were close," Lucy asked, the distress over her aunt clear.

"There's not much to tell. She's looking for something. I had little to do with it. Maybe if I'd been here, she would be back by now."

"You can hardly be blamed for dying!" Lucy cried.

"No, but I can blame whoever tried to kill me."

"What happened to you? Did someone hurt you?" Lucy asked, wide eyed, finally testing the tea.

"No. They saved me," Stelle whispered into the cup. "So it was boring?"

"Terribly. I thought of talking to Dr Moss about Aunt Daye, but he's on Orion, not the Obsidian," Lucy continued. Stelle startled at the mention of Dr Moss but tried to not let it show.

"Why Dr Moss?" Stelle asked, turning the glass in her hands.

"Oh, I was talking to Wynter, who said something about Lady Daye and an old connection between her and Dr Moss. But Wynter got suspicious of my questions, and that was all I could find out. Although you should see the dresses she made for me. Do you remember when the most interesting thing was our dresses?"

Stelle sighed. That felt like a lifetime ago.

Thirty-Five

Sleep came in fits and waves, and when Stelle woke, she was tired. Unwelcome thoughts of Merrick and the Lark intruded. She hoped he'd made it safely off the base. She wondered if Ruse was still a threat. She wanted Merrick.

Rummaging through her cupboards, she found a tea kettle, but didn't actually want tea, and instead tried to take it apart. She stripped off the socket where it attached to the wall and pulled off random bits. She was surprised to be able to break it down into so many pieces. When she was finished, she tucked it all away into a drawer.

Without her own kettle, she would have to request tea. She went without, and the lack caused a dull ache behind her tired eyes.

The Inkton family arrived at the castle. With Violet as the guest of honour, they had the entire north wing. If they were aware of her presence, none of them came to see her.

Perhaps they didn't know.

Her stomach was tied in knots. The evening's dinner was the first of the formal events and would be followed by a grand ball the next night.

Dinner would be the first time she'd see her family since they'd pronounced her dead. A public arena for such an encounter shouldn't have been a comfort, but it was. Stelle didn't know what to expect, but grand hugs and displays of emotion would not be it.

Getting ready, she opted for a coronet of braids. They wound around the back of her head and collected into a single long braid. It rested over her shoulder. She was strengthened to carry her hair the way Dowswell had. The added rubies made it soft and stunning. The gown Lucy had given her needed little adjustment. Stelle had stood in silence as she was pinned and stitched into it. Red—like the one she had left in.

"A little more at the bottom, please," Stelle asked, not even caring that she had said please.

The seamstresses worked swiftly, then left her alone to finish dressing.

Once ready, she walked down the hallway unescorted. Her family was in the north wing and hadn't summoned her. And Lucy, now playing the part of hostess in Lady Daye's absence, would already be there.

Her hand trembled on the rail as she descended the stairs leading to the back terrace dining room.

The sun, already low, sent a warm glow over the flower beds, and soft feathers danced in tall vases and ran in garlands over bannisters.

The room lacked a certain level of discomfort that Lady Daye always imposed on such events. It was light and pretty—much like Lucy. Valtine was a beautiful, peaceful place to live; it was the people who chose to make it miserable.

Stelle thought of her own dreariness and the entitlement that clung to her.

She stood outside the dining area and watched her friend before entering. Lucy was draped regally in a silvery-pink gown. She had a quick smile and a silly comment for everyone who passed by, putting everyone at ease.

"Well, at least you don't *look* compromised."

Stelle turned around to face her mother, who had come up behind her.

"Mother," Stelle said calmly and picked at the edge of her glove. Her heart was hammering in her chest. Her mother looked stunning in a gown dripping with gems and glass diamonds. It must have weighed a ton.

"Don't pick at your glove. People might assume something is wrong," Lady Inkton said.

The comfortable stone wall coiled up and enclosed her heart.

"What could be wrong about coming back from the dead?" Stelle asked, letting her hands fall to her side as she strode into the dining room. As far as family greetings went, the moment hadn't been terrible.

Lord Inkton followed behind them and looked as though he wanted to rush to Stelle's side, but he held back the outward display of emotion.

Lucy greeted her, and Lord Daye raised Stelle's hand and placed a kiss in the air above her wrist.

The room pretended to carry on with conversation, but all eyes were on her. She wandered around, making polite conversation, daring anyone to approach her, and was relieved when the dinner bell sounded.

Her sister, Lady Violet, sat at the head of the table between her mother and father. Lady Claire's place remained beside Lady Violet, but Stelle was beside her. Almost at the head of the table.

Everyone except Lucy looked uncomfortable with the seating. No one knew what to do. So much silliness over an Idex; she wondered how long she should pretend to care. Stelle let out a strangled laugh, which awarded her a sharp look from her mother.

The wall she had put up cracked. It was there, but not strong like it once was. As if everything everyone said threatened to split it open.

Lady Violet shifted uncomfortably in her chair and glared at her. Small glasses of haze were brought out after dinner. Stelle looked between her sister and the other guests. The person who'd tried to have her killed might be in this very room.

Lady Claire downed hers quickly. Stelle hated the sight of the stuff. When she was certain no one was looking, she switched glasses, placing the empty one in front of herself, and then patted Lady Claire on the hand.

"I apologize for taking your rooms. Apparently, coming back from the dead is an inconvenience for everyone." Stelle meant it kindly. Lady Claire took the offered glass of haze and returned the fake smile.

"I am curious—as is everyone—where you were…"

"Curiosity isn't a virtue," Stelle said, mimicking her mother's tone.

Lucy beamed from across the table, unaware of the drama unfolding in front of her.

It was all too much. Too many cracks, too many pieces of

her left all over the place. Too much to hold together. The whole charade was so unbelievably silly. All this pretence over an organic compound added to her DNA. It didn't make her better or worse than anyone.

This was all she was good for—making polite conversation at parties and hosting events so that society could function. A serving of cortivals and wine was placed in front of her. She loved the delicacy, but having them in front of her now was too much.

"If you must know, Lady Claire," Stelle said her name loudly and clearly enough for anyone to listen in and hear them. "I fell in love with a salvage captain. He drives a lovely bin collecting the craziest things. You wouldn't believe what gets left out in space!"

"Enough, Lady Cristelle. I think perhaps this whole evening is a bit much. Perhaps you are ready to retire for the evening." Lady Inkton waved her hand.

"I'm actually rejuvenated by such a lovely welcome home." Stelle grinned wildly at all the guests but after her brief outburst dutifully remained quiet for the rest of the meal.

Lucy announced dessert out on the veranda. As they rose and exited the dining room, Stelle was sure everyone was waiting for her to make another mistake. The dress was strung too tight, and her feet longed for her floppy red slippers.

Once outside, Stelle breathed in the fresh air, held a plate of cakes in one hand, and leaned over the white stone railing. The stars twinkled above them. Lavender and jasmine softened the air.

"Why did you have to come back?" Lady Violet asked, joining her at the railing.

"Sorry to disappoint."

"You don't even like it here. Not the way I do. I have plans for the estates. Mother knows I would be a better heiress."

"Sounds like you've been thinking a lot about it in only a few months."

"Unlike you, I've been thinking about it my whole life."

Stelle looked at her sister. She had always assumed she was weak, incapable of handling the pressures of Valtine. But there was something else in the way she spoke.

"Mother is waiting for one wrong move to have you banned from Valtine. All the rumours after the Monrovia were horrid. Mother was so mad that you came to the castle. She thought you should have done the right thing and stayed out of sight. This messes everything up!"

"You know nothing about the Monrovia, or what happened afterward. None of you do." Stelle tossed the cakes off the railing, raining them down onto the gardens below. Everyone but her family wanted to know the truth. They didn't care where she'd been or what she'd been doing. They only cared that she was making a mess of their perfect plans.

"Don't talk to me like that. I know more than you think I do," Lady Violet preened and took a bite of her cake.

"What do you know?" Stelle demanded, grabbing Violet's arm. Stelle hadn't slipped up, but there was the ever-lingering fear that she would do or say something that would expose the Lark.

Lady Violet wrenched her arm free. "Leave me alone, or I'm going to scream! I'll tell everyone you're deranged from living in a safety pod. Then they'll never let you be heiress."

"How do you know about the safety pod?" Stelle studied her

sister. There was no way she could know about Stelle being on the pod. The reason she hadn't been found and declared dead was that no one knew she was out there, and she had been very careful to not mention it. "If you don't tell me what you're hiding, I'll do whatever it takes to make sure you never get a single coin from my lands when I inherit. Violet, what did you do? Five people died on the Monrovia—six, if you count me."

Lady Violet started to cry. Stelle wasn't sure if it was the threat to take away income or the fact that people had died, but all at once her sister looked very small.

"You hated it here. I don't know why you hated all of us so much. People work hard to get here and have a peaceful life. It can be so beautiful and… they said you would be happy. That you'd have everything you ever wanted. I paid to make sure you'd be safe and very, very far away. They promised you'd never return."

Lady Violet stopped talking as a couple walked past them. To anyone looking on, it would appear to be estranged sisters catching up after months lost, not the admittance of ultimate betrayal. Stelle felt like someone had punched her in the stomach. All the air whooshed out of her. Her fingers wrapped around the railing.

No one would have guessed that Lady Violet was in part responsible for the Monrovia. If ever there was a secret to be kept, this was it. It wouldn't only ruin Lady Violet, but likely the whole family.

"Lord Kent won't want to marry me if I'm not heiress."

"Lord Kent? What does he have to do with it? He's the least of your concerns right now." Stelle knew her sister was sheltered and spoiled, but her concern over Lord Kent and not the lives lost was not the sister she thought she knew.

"No one was supposed to die. What are you going to do?" Lady Violet asked. Stelle thought through all the things Merrick had told her about her pod. It had been designed to be sent off into space. Perhaps what Violet was saying was true. Someone was going to pick her up and make her disappear. But Violet had to have known that would cause a ten-year delay. However, being named heiress was different than actually being one, and her mother was still very much alive. Ten years wouldn't be a long wait at all. The explosion hadn't been planned though, and people had died. If word got out as to what had really happened, more questions would surface, and the Lark could be in danger.

"There isn't anything either of us can do. I'm not dead, but my Idex is. And there's a ball tomorrow to prepare for."

"You came back crazy."

"Yes, perhaps a little. We need to have dessert, and then sleep—and you need to never say the word 'Monrovia' to anyone, ever again. Do you understand?"

Lady Violet nodded her head.

And then there was nothing more to say. Stelle couldn't look at her sister, not after what she'd intended to do to her. At least now she wouldn't be afraid, waiting for an unexpected assassin to pop up. Stelle wished she could talk to Merrick, or even Jasper, and tell them she was safe. She wished she could talk to Ava.

Stelle left the party without telling anyone—Lucy would understand if she didn't want to be there.

When sleep didn't claim her, she made her way through the empty halls. Soft floor lights in the stone lit up in front of her as she passed doors and paintings and open windows.

She had been so terrible that no one had wanted her back. She didn't want to be back. Perhaps, in time, things would be different.

Instead of going back to her room, she made her way down to the kitchens. She let herself in and rummaged for a tea pot.

Thirty-Six

Stelle sat in the empty kitchens. She wondered if anyone had stopped the alerts that were jamming the systems every time she entered a room.

The kitchen was enormous, and two cupboards in, she'd abandoned her search. Someone would be down shortly.

She traced the silver lines that swirled on the smooth surface of the table, the cold stone beneath her warm fingertips. Merrick was hopefully on a new adventure, or picking through space junk. Their lives were forever apart.

Stelle's father walked into the kitchen, startling her. Long evening robes made him look old and round. "Your mother sent me down to make sure you didn't dismantle anything else. She doesn't want any more servants to talk of tea pots in drawers."

It sounded like a rebuke, but he grinned and sat down on a chair across from her. Reaching across the white marble table, he held her hand. "It's good to have you home," he said.

"Well, at least someone will say it." It felt nice to be greeted after the day of silence.

"Do not judge your mother harshly. She cannot formally accept you until all of this is resolved; to do so could put your sister's future in jeopardy should it be decided your time away was less than acceptable. She doesn't want to shun you—but no one knows what happened to you."

Stelle pulled her hands back and stood. He was being kind, but he was also looking for a truth she couldn't give him. A truth she would never give anyone.

She walked through the long expanse of the room and looked out the back window into the gardens. Fruit trees and vegetable beds and all kinds of berries sat in perfect rows in perfect greenhouses. The golden leaves rustled in the wind, catching the moonlight like flickering golden coins.

It was peaceful and beautiful

"I'm sorry, Dad. I can't tell you."

He puttered around the kitchen until he found two tall glasses and then opened a bottom cupboard, pulling out a dark grey bottle.

"Not haze—please," Stelle said, wrinkling her nose.

He put the grey bottle back and pulled out a dark-red glass decanter. He poured hers half full of the wine and handed it to her. She took a sip, her mouth puckering at the heavy flavour.

"I'm sorry, I shouldn't have pushed you so hard to follow the cargo. Or even what happened with Captain Ward... I thought Captain Ward would give you a life away from here." He swirled his wine around and up the sides, then let it settle back into the glass.

She hadn't thought much about Captain Ward. Her father had been insistent that she make an offer. The whole situation had worked out in her favour, because she had other business on the Obsidian, and it had provided an excellent cover for what she'd actually been doing. For a brief moment during her time on the luxury cargo ship she'd entertained thoughts of a simple life being married to Captain Ward. He was nice enough, but in love with Wynter—and knew she would never have actually gotten between them.

"You wanted me gone too?" Stelle asked.

He sighed. His shoulders drooped from the weight of his evening cloak.

"Most people on Valtine work. They have farms or are servants in grand houses. There are guilds here, although not like on Orion. There are perfume houses and vacation resorts. There are miners and engineers. There are some of the best academics and teachers."

"And I am a spoiled brat—" Stelle interjected.

"You learned music, dance and etiquette and how to keep our family's Idex line perfect. You learned the politics of land ownership, and your mother has been pushing you to make an offer for several gentlemen. I always imagined you for something else."

Stelle wondered what she would have done if she hadn't been an heiress.

"Perhaps a tea server?" Stelle mused.

"We were not meant to be waited on hand and foot, or to have our every move scrutinized. The pressure is not the same for everyone, and you had your own particularly destructive way of dealing with it."

"So you wanted me gone." Stelle finished her wine and set the glass down.

"Yes, but for your sake as well as ours." His eyes twinkled.

He pulled a small screen card out of his pocket, along with a stack of papers and a metal medallion. Its jewel mosaic perfume bottle was set into white onyx.

"When I found out you were still alive, I finished this. It's the guild-deeds to the perfumery. They belong to you now. The funds are in your name. I came into my marriage with guild status. They shunned your mother for a time. I promised her I could fit in, and I did. We raised you to do both. With this, no one will deny your land inheritance when your time comes. For now, you have access to an astounding fortune. I know you'll mind it well, and our family will become powerful beyond what your mother and I ever dreamed. I am happy to say I am legally passing it all to you and have now become entirely dependent on your mother."

"Mother is going to be furious. The guilds will be furious," Stelle said, running her hand over the beautiful necklace. She instinctively reached for the braided wires she still wore on a chain around her neck. Balls and parties wouldn't be the half of what she could do. At once, all the feelings of uselessness fled. Her father was right—she wasn't meant for this life—but this life had been given to her. Dr Moss had provided a cure, Jasper the connections, Merrick the tech, and Sers and Lavalle had the heart to keep flying. She had unlimited wealth, access to cargo ships, and little vials of perfume that could carry anything anywhere, including little bottles of the cure. She would find the Lark, no matter how long it took—and she would put the wealth of Valtine behind it.

It was a political move. By making her wealthy with the guilds in her own right, her father had ensured that no one would refuse her the place of heiress of the land on Valtine.

Both sides would seek to leverage the situation. Stelle knew now more than ever how much they both wanted power. And she planned to do something entirely different with it. Holding it, the path forward was laid out for her.

If she played everything perfectly, the control they would have—the income she would have—was staggering. She'd find a way to help Merrick and the Lark, even if not directly. With this, she could do anything.

"Once this comes out, everyone will forget you were missing." He patted her hand and left the kitchen.

Everyone would politely forget she had been dead. Everyone except her.

Thirty-Seven

Stelle readied herself for the ball. A new gold gown had arrived from Wynter only an hour before. An accompanying note was scrawled across a slip of paper that read, *I'm happy you're not dead*. The dress spilled to the floor; a narrow slit rose just above her knee, sleeves scooped off her shoulders and went slinking down her arms.

Over the course of one day, everything had changed. It became known that Stelle was now a guild owner.

The ball that was supposed to mark her sister's acceptance as heiress was crafted into an engagement party between Lady Violet and Lord Kent. Despite Violet's fears that he wouldn't want her unless she was an heiress, he had proposed and saved the day. It was embarrassing the way her family gushed over him, as if he was the one who had only just arrived back from the dead.

Despite being hasty, Stelle wondered if it wasn't a terrible match. Lord Kent had certainly talked about Violet constantly when they were on the Monrovia.

Stelle met her family at the ballroom entrance.

Lady Violet wore a soft-pink gown wrapped in lace. Lord Kent had matching roses attached to the cuffs of his long jacket.

Her mother wore a blue dress that looked like a waterfall with a swish of white ruffles billowing around the hem. She was less than pleased to see her as she took her place and entered the ballroom. Lucy had transformed it into a midnight paradise. Black drapes swept from the ceiling and covered the pillars. Glittering gems sparkled against the fire-like orbs that hovered high over the dance floor.

The guests all acted accordingly. The whispers that crept around the edge of the room were silenced with stern looks. No one wanted to be out of favour, and everyone wanted to be there. The packed room was suffocating. Stelle wanted to laugh at the absurdity of it. They all knew the ball was for Lady Violet's now-failed promotion. They all knew it was a lie, and yet every single person in the room acted as if nothing was out of sorts.

"You will be on your best behaviour tonight. This entire business could have been avoided if you had come home quietly. Do not drink too much haze and not one word about pirates."

"Of course, Mother," Stelle said, leaving her family to join the dancers.

As she danced, she kept her conversation light and friendly, laughing exactly when she should, all the while with an aching heart. She would give almost anything to be dancing with Merrick on the Lark—she would have even accepted dancing with Jasper.

Once she had smiled and accepted the correct number of

dances, she made her way to the balcony. Before she could get a moment of peace, she was roughly pulled to the side.

"Lord Kent—" Stelle said, surprised. There was a wariness of constantly being abducted, captured, or in need of rescue. "What could you possibly want? Are my jewels not acceptable tonight?"

"I want you to disappear again. I want you to refuse your title and disappear to an island. Don't you realize how many lives you're ruining?"

Stelle's eyes narrowed on him. He grabbed her arm and dug his fingers in. He wasn't so boring now.

"I have guild status," Stelle countered, pulling her arm back but it only increased the strength of his grip.

"I have this." Lord Kent held up a small datafile. "Every detail of your sister's *involvement* with the Monrovia."

The datafile was a small chip. Anything could be on it. But if he was willing to threaten her with it, perhaps he wasn't bluffing. Either way, Lord Kent knowing about Violet's involvement was concerning. How did he know? Stelle thought back to the Monrovia. Lord Kent had known her movements and that she had left the dinner. He hadn't followed her, but it was possible he'd had someone else push her into the pod. It had been ridiculous to assume that her sister had planned it on her own.

"Involvement you encouraged?" Stelle asked, arching her brow. She let her arm relax under his grip, showing him she was unafraid. He tucked the chip into the inside pocket of his jacket and shrugged, confirming her suspicions.

A wave of protectiveness toward her sister welled up despite the irreparable rift between them and she wanted nothing more than to drop Lord Kent.

He pulled her close and grabbed her other arm. "Disappear, or maybe you'd consider an engagement to me. You were always fond of me. Either way, I will have access to Valtine courts."

Lord Kent pulled her arms until she was close, then leaned down to force a kiss. Stelle allowed herself a moment to roll her eyes before pushing her full weight at him. He stumbled back a step, releasing one of her arms. Taking the moment of leverage, she put all of her weight into one leg and thrust her knee up into his stomach.

Stelle took a step back into another solid mass. A blade flicked in her periphery and pressed against Lord Kent's neck.

"I suggest you take an extended vacation away from Valtine," the man beside her said.

"I'll ruin them—" his voice trembled as he got a good look at Jasper—Lord Terrington. His eyes grew wide with fear, and his bravado faltered.

"With this?" Stelle asked, holding up the datachip she'd swiped from his pocket during the altercation. The blade flicked closed. "Without proof, no one will believe you."

Stelle's heart was pounding as Lord Kent made a hasty escape. She held the chip out to Jasper.

"What are you doing here?" she asked. Jasper was wearing a fine Valtine suit with navy-and-gold trim that reminded her of the chairs on the bridge of the Lark.

"Someone said they saw you go outside."

"No, here… on Valtine. Is Merrick… is he okay?" Stelle had never considered he wouldn't make it off the moonbase, but what if Jasper hadn't gotten to him quickly enough? What if he had died? Jasper wouldn't be here unless something had gone very wrong.

"We miscalculated in our plan—a flaw Lavalle pointed out the moment I returned—with Merrick," he said, knowing his delay on Merrick's safety rankled her. "Your Idex was scanned, but so was mine. It was too much of a coincidence that two from Valtine would be on the moonbase at the same time without an explanation. Perhaps we should have this conversation somewhere else. You are going to be missed from the party—and since Lord Kent will now also be missing, it's best you not be missing at the same time." He sounded lofty and not at all like the Jasper she remembered.

Stelle wanted to scream but took Jasper's hand. They made their way back into the ballroom as if nothing had happened.

The music slowed. They stood at the edge of the dance floor as the dance came to an end. Stelle heard the ripple of gossip run through the room. Like a wave it swelled, the name Lord Terrington on everyone's lips. She closed her eyes and rubbed her brow with her hand. This was exhausting. When she opened her eyes, she didn't want to make eye contact with anyone and stared at the floor, trying to regain her composure. Jasper commented on the decor and the orchestra and said nothing of Merrick or his purpose there.

When the music started, Jasper led her to the dance floor. The orchestra provided them with the chance to talk quietly as they moved around the couples. Jasper was an expert dancer, as Stelle remembered from the Lark, but there was a sadness in his eyes as he led her that wasn't there the last time they had danced.

"There is gossip going around that I rescued you after the

Monrovia. You spent the last few moons convincing me I should return to Valtine. That was why we were on the moonbase together—and why you exposed yourself—you had given up on me. It's a rumour that protects the Lark and keeps us well out of the way of an investigation into the death of a man named Ruse. That could be it, if you want. It could stop there. Merrick wanted you to have a choice before he came in and ruined your reputation. There could also be a rumour that you met up with my cousin along the way—"

"Where is he?"

"He's not really my cousin—he's a poor mechanic from Koros—but no one needs to know that."

"Where is he?" Stelle stopped dancing in the middle of the floor. Other couples had to take long steps to get around them, trying to catch what they were saying. All eyes were on her and Jasper. Her heart hammered in her chest. Jasper looked over her shoulder, focusing on something near the door.

Stelle followed his gaze across the ballroom to where Merrick was waiting for her. He looked devastatingly handsome in formal attire.

The orchestra stopped, and the guests quickly moved out of the way as Stelle lifted the hem of her skirt and broke into a run, brushing past gasping gossips. She threw herself into Merrick's arms, grabbed his smoothly shaved chin, and kissed him. Then kissed him again. And one more time to make sure he was really and truly there, and that everyone in the ballroom saw it.

"I love you. I love you, and I thought I'd never see you again." Her voice carried through the ballroom.

There were gasps and swoons around the room. The room

spun with gossip—some true, some not. She spied her mother out of the corner of her eye. She was frantically trying to get news of who her daughter/heiress/Inkton owner was kissing. Stelle truly didn't care. Her heart was fluttering and her mind spinning.

Merrick released her and stepped back a little. He looked at her from head to toe as if he were assessing a problem to be fixed. He lifted her hand, kissed the inside of her wrist, and said, "There's the terrible gossip going around that you and Lord Terrington have somewhat of an affection for one another. I think it best we set the record straight. Stelle—I love you."

A gasp went up from the crowd.

"That's Lady Cristelle," she said, taking her hand back and kissing him one more time.

Lucy motioned for the orchestra to start playing, and the dance continued.

Merrick swept Stelle onto the floor.

"I'm no longer in danger," Stelle said, almost a little self conscious and worried for the briefest moment that it was what had drawn them all back. The gold in her dress shimmered as they spun under the lights, and she quietly explained what had happened with her sister and Lord Kent.

"How is it possible you're here?" Stelle asked when she finished her own tale.

"We ran into some difficulty explaining Lord Terrington's Idex on the base and reached out to an old friend. I think you mentioned him in some of your stories—a Captain Ward? That and we were all worried about your safety. With the Idex system down temporarily, anyone can get into these parties."

Merrick nodded to where Sers and Lavalle leaned against the bar that ran along the far wall. They were decked out in Valtine finery like big shots. Beside them Wynter and Captain Ward stood listening intently to the co-pilots as they told their stories—some of them probably true, some of them less accurate.

"And I knew I had to see you again—I had to at least try. Ava once told me that one day, I'd need someone to rescue me, and when that day came, I should go for it."

Thirty-Eight

The day after the ball, Lady Violet blamed Stelle for her broken engagement with Lord Kent. He left Valtine with only a brief note delivered to Lady Violet. Stelle abandoned attempts to comfort the spoiled girl. She was better off without him, and Stelle could only hope that one day she would see that.

The Obsidian and Inkton cargo was waiting for them. Captain Ward had expressed his appreciation for the cargo but was wary of bringing Stelle back onto his ship. Now that they had funds and access to new ways of moving information and medical supplies, they'd have to reorganize. The best place to do that was on Orion and with Dr Moss's help.

Sers and Lavalle were taking the Lark to Orion ahead of them. Jasper claimed he had another matter to attend to, one that he had to do as Lord Terrington. No one dared to ask questions.

Lucy sat on the edge of Stelle's bed, one foot swinging back and forth.

"I can get someone to do that for you," Lucy said, looking at the half-empty trunk. But Stelle wanted to pack them herself. She packed her own trunks on Koros and could do it here too.

"You could come with us," Stelle said. Lifting the trunk, she brought it to the door of her room and pushed it into the hall.

"With Aunt Daye missing, my uncle still refuses to let me leave, and… I need to find her. Or at least what happened to her."

Stelle told Lucy what little she knew of her aunt. She remembered befriending Mme Helix, sending messages and going to all the effort to make sure Lady Daye got what she wanted. She knew Lady Daye had planned to leave after that, but she had never told Stelle where she was going.

"Lucy, I don't know much, but I don't think she wants to be found," Stelle said, trying to reassure her friend.

There was a knock at the door. Stelle opened it to a waiting Merrick.

Lucy hugged her tightly. "I wish you could stay. It's so boring when you're not here."

After the farewell, Lucy strolled down the hall and out of sight.

"I'm ready if the Obsidian is," Stelle said, taking a final look around the room.

Merrick paused, holding her hand. He looked down at her.

"Why are you looking at me like that?" Stelle asked, tugging on his arm, a blush rushing to her cheeks. He tucked a wisp of hair behind her ear, sending a trill down her spine. Stelle had grown up believing love was not for someone like her. It was out of reach and unattainable. She never imagined she would love someone as much as she loved Merrick. It was a wonder that he loved her in return.

"I was just thinking how very thankful I am."

"That we get to spend the next few moons on a proper cargo ship?"

"No, I was thinking how thankful I am that you were lost between the stars."

Wynter sat on a black carpet in what used to be Dr Moss's room. Stacks of journals, notes, and charts were scattered around her. She'd arranged them into piles by date, going back twenty years noticing the increase around the time Ward's uncle died. Then she sorted them by location. There were no datapads or electronic files. Everything was handwritten.

Wynter jumped as the door behind her opened.

"I need a moment of your time," Lady Cristelle said, entering the room.

"How did you find me?" Wynter asked. Lady Cristelle was wearing a black and navy dress that was incredibly formal for an ordinary day on the Obsidian. She waved her hand absently as if it was obvious how she'd found Wynter. Reaching into her pocket, she took out a folded envelope.

"Dr Moss wanted me to give this to you if I ever saw you again. I'm sorry it took so long, but it's not as if we spend time in each other's company."

In the week Lady Cristelle and Merrick had been on the Obsidian, Wynter had done her best to avoid her. If she was being honest with herself, she was also avoiding Ward. He had been acting strange ever since Valtine—secretive. It's how she'd ended up in Dr Moss's untouched rooms and how she'd found all the journals in the hidden compartment behind his bookshelf. Now she had a few secrets of her own.

Wynter took the envelope and held it to her chest.

"When did you see Dr Moss?"

"That is not a question I can answer," she replied. She looked at the stacks and back at Wynter. "You should probably move those to a more secure location. What if the new doctor decides he wants to use Dr Moss's rooms?"

It was funny that everyone referred to them as Dr Moss's rooms. But she was right—whatever these were, they weren't safe here. He'd been gone for some time and eventually the primary medical staff might want to use the somber den.

"I'll help you, but it's best after this that we keep our distance from one another. I might need to leave suddenly and it's best if there's a plausible reason—like if I stormed off in a huff because of something you said. It's all dramatic—I know —and perhaps there's a place for us to truly be friends in the future. Or not. I can understand why. I'll go find something large enough to move these."

As quickly as she'd arrived, she was gone, leaving Wynter spinning. Unfolding the note, Wynter recognized Dr Moss's handwriting.

Wynter. I need you to do something for me...